Revenge R Us

Look out for more books in the Goosebumps Series 2000
by R.L. Stine:

1 *Cry of the Cat*
2 *Bride of the Living Dummy*
3 *Creature Teacher*
4 *Invasion of the Body Squeezers, Part 1*
5 *Invasion of the Body Squeezers, Part 2*
6 *I Am Your Evil Twin*
8 *Fright Camp*
9 *Are You Terrified Yet?*

Revenge R Us

R.L. Stine

Hippo

Scholastic Children's Books
Commonwealth House, 1–19 New Oxford Street, London WC1A 1NU, UK
a division of Scholastic Ltd
London ~ New York ~ Toronto ~ Sydney ~ Auckland
Mexico City ~ New Delhi ~ Hong Kong

First published in the USA by Scholastic Inc., 1998
First published in the UK by Scholastic Ltd, 1999

ISBN 0 590 11402 6

Typeset by Rowland Phototypesetting Ltd, Bury St Edmunds, Suffolk
Printed by Mackays of Chatham plc, Chatham, Kent.

10 9 8 7 6 5 4 3 2 1

Wade Brill.

I wrote my name with one finger in the steam on my bathroom mirror. Then I wiped it away with a bath towel.

The room was still steamy and hot from my shower. I gazed at myself in the mirror. I started to brush my short brownish-blonde hair. Then I carefully tucked my fringe back with a hair-clip.

I suppose I'll wear my new white sun-dress to Erin's birthday party, I decided. And the white sandals.

Erin's party was supposed to be a barbecue. But behind me, I could hear the rain pounding against my bedroom window.

I don't care, I decided. The white sun-dress is my coolest outfit. I'll just pretend it's sunny and hot out.

I hurried into my room to get dressed. I didn't want to be late for the party. Rain drummed against the window, nearly drowning out the voices on the TV on my dressing-table.

I grabbed the sun-dress and pulled it off the hanger. The film on TV caught my attention: *Revenge of the Worm People*.

I'd already seen it. It was really stupid—about these worms who grow very tall and attack a fishing village because they don't want to be used as bait.

But I'll watch anything with the word *revenge* in the title. I think about revenge a lot.

You would too—if you had my brother.

Micah Brill. That's his name. Micah, spelled C-R-E-E-P.

Micah is seventeen, five years older than me. He's tall and wavy-haired, and good-looking, and you'd think he'd pick on someone his own size. But he's been torturing me since the day I was born.

He doesn't just tease me. He tricks me. He treats me as a slave. He embarrasses me in front of my friends.

Last week, a group of my friends were over. We were watching a video. *Revenge of the Shadow Creatures*. I told you. I'll watch anything with *revenge* in the title!

My friend Carl Jeffers was over. And my friend Julie Wilson and her brother Steve.

I admit it. I have a crush on Steve. He's an eighth grader, and he's really cool. So I was trying to be cool too.

But of course Micah ruined everything.

2

He came prancing into the living-room during the best part of the film. "Yo, rugrats! How do you like my new hat?"

Ready for a laugh? Micah was wearing my underwear on his head. An old pair of pink knickers that Aunt Claire had given me. With MONDAY printed across the bottom.

My friends laughed. I could feel my face growing hot. I knew I was blushing beet-red. Micah danced round the room, shaking the underwear in everyone's face, enjoying himself.

"Wade—are you wearing 'Wednesday' today?" Julie teased.

Ha ha.

"Let's check!" Micah cried. He pounced on me and tried to pull my shorts down.

"Get off me, you freak!" I shouted. I butted his stomach as hard as I could with my head.

That slowed him down a little. He tore the underwear off and threw it to Steve.

YAAAIIII! How's that for a Kodak Moment? A boy I like sitting there with my knickers in his hands!

Life with Micah is a laugh a minute.

He's always going through my dressing-table drawers. Always snooping round my room. And I know why. He's searching for my diary.

But he can't find it. I have a secret hiding-place for it. I won't let Micah embarrass me with my diary. I won't.

3

Micah is always borrowing my stuff without telling me. Once, he took two of my favourite CDs and *gave* them to a friend of his!

He does everything he can to make my life miserable. He knows I'm not as good a student as he is. He knows I have to study really hard.

So what does he do? Every time I have to study for a test, he cranks up his stereo as loud as it will go.

Sometimes I just want to scream.

Don't get me started about Micah. I can go on and on . . .

Once Mum told Micah he couldn't go out on Saturday night until he'd cleaned his room. He's seventeen, and he just throws his stuff on the floor like a two-year-old.

"Wade, do me a big favour," he whispered. "If you clean my room, I'll pay you twenty-five dollars."

Well, I could really use twenty-five dollars. Who couldn't? So I cleaned his disgusting room—and it wasn't easy, believe me. It was like cleaning a *swamp*. I even found a dead mouse under the bed, all decayed and yucky.

It took me all day. Mum inspected his room, patted Micah on the back, and told him he'd done a great job.

After she'd gone downstairs, I demanded my money. "Pay up, Micah. Twenty-five big ones."

He stared at me as if I was crazy. "Twenty-five

dollars?" he cried. "Where would I get twenty-five dollars?" And he ran out to meet his friends.

Could I complain to my parents?

No way. They think he's perfect.

He gets straight A's. He's captain of the varsity soccer team. And he'll probably get a full scholarship to college.

Big deal, right? That doesn't mean he's *human*!

Sometimes I try to complain about him. When Mum got home from the supermarket the other day, I greeted her at the door. "Mum—Micah went through my dressing-table again. He came out in front of my friends wearing my underwear on his head!"

Mum laughed. "Your brother is *so* funny!" She pushed past me to the kitchen to put away the groceries.

"But Mum—" I protested.

"He only teases you because he likes you," Mum called back to me.

Yeah. Right. I really believe that.

My brother is a complete super-sized pain. That's why I watch *revenge* films.

But I didn't have time to watch TV. I had to get ready for Erin's party.

As I sat on the edge of my bed and started to pull on my white sandals, I had no idea that I was minutes away from the worst day of my life.

And maybe the best . . .

"But why can't *you* drive me to the party?"

I was following Mum from the bedroom to the bathroom to the bedroom again while she finished dressing. She and Dad had a hospital banquet to go to. My dad is a doctor.

"We're not driving," Mum replied. "Dr Tolbert is picking us up."

"Micah has the car," Dad chimed in. He was struggling with his tie. "I told you, he'll drive you to your party."

"But Micah is still at the gym!" I protested. "He was supposed to be back here half an hour ago!"

"He won't forget you," Dad said.

I rolled my eyes. Micah has only forgotten about me a thousand times. This week.

Mum snapped a bracelet over her wrist and checked herself in the mirror. Then she gave me a quick kiss. "Enjoy Erin's party. What a shame it's pouring."

I heard Dr Tolbert honk his horn. I stared out

6

of the window as my parents drove away in the rain.

Where is Micah? I wondered angrily. Where *is* he?

I checked myself in the mirror for the hundredth time. Then I started to pace to and fro. As I paced, I watched the numbers click by on my digital clock radio.

6:20 . . . 6:21 . . . 6:22 . . .

I was fuming! Erin's party had already started. That stupid Micah!

He's probably still at the gym, I figured. Playing basketball with his buddies, having forgotten all about me.

Or he's remembered, and he doesn't care.

I'm going to miss the party. I'm going to miss the whole thing.

I'm going to explode. I'm so angry, I'm going to explode!

"YAAAAIIIII!" I let out a shrill scream. I had to do something.

Then I grabbed the phone and called my friend Carl. He lives on the next block. He could pick me up.

His mother answered. "Oh, I'm sorry, Wade. I dropped Carl off at Erin's house at least half an hour ago."

Of course. Carl was already at the party. He didn't have to depend on Micah. Micah, spelled J-E-R-K.

Can I walk to Erin's house? I asked myself. I stared out at the pounding rain. No. Too far.

The gym was closer. Only four blocks away.

I'll walk to the gym and get Micah, I decided.

I glanced down at my white sandals. A little rain won't hurt them, I thought. I'm not going far.

I grabbed an umbrella and stepped out into the rain. I started down the driveway. "Ohhh." I uttered a low moan as cold water splashed over my feet. I'd stepped into a deep puddle.

I gritted my teeth and sloshed down the street. A river of water gushed along the kerb. I braced my umbrella against the wind.

Then *R R I I I-P!* **A** powerful blast of wind slashed my umbrella—and flipped it inside out.

Rain swept over me like an ocean wave. In a second, I was drenched from fringe to sandals.

"Micah!" I growled. "I'm going to *kill* you for this!"

I dropped my umbrella in a rubbish bin and forged ahead. My hair was plastered to my face. My sun-dress stuck wetly to my skin.

I trudged another block. Then I saw the car roaring towards me.

I didn't have time to cry out. Or jump away from the kerb.

The car shot up beside me. Squealed to a stop—sending up a high spray of water. A tidal wave of water and mud!

8

It splattered over me, cold and thick.

"Ohhhh." Sputtering, I staggered backwards. I wiped the glop out of my eyes with both hands.

"My dress!' I shrieked. Drenched. Drenched with gloppy brown mud.

The driver of the car rolled down his window. "Need a lift?"

Micah!

He threw back his head and laughed. His dark eyes flashed gleefully.

"You—you—you *creep*!" I screeched. "Look what you did to me! I'm telling Mum and Dad!"

"Telling them what?" he demanded, still grinning. "It was an accident. I didn't see that mud puddle there."

"You did it on purpose!" I screeched. "I'll tell Mum and Dad you were driving like a maniac. They'll never let you have a car of your own!"

That's Micah's dream. He wants his own car more than anything. He's been giving swimming lessons at the town pool this summer, saving every penny for a car.

Micah shrugged. "Accidents happen."

He reached out of the car window and pinched my cheek. I tried to bite his fingers. Then I got into the car. I mean, what else could I do?

I fumed silently all the way to Erin's house. Micah dropped me off at the bottom of the driveway. I climbed out and slammed the door furiously without saying goodbye.

9

"Have fun," Micah sneered. "And by the way—you look great!"

He squealed off—and splashed me again!

I trudged up to the front door. I could hear kids laughing and talking inside. Water ran down my forehead. I could barely see the doorbell.

Erin opened the door, and her jaw dropped. "Wade! What happened?"

"Don't ask," I muttered.

"I like your brown sun-dress," she said.

"Funny," I growled. "Ha ha. Do you have anything you can lend me?"

I followed her up to her room. She handed me a T-shirt and a pair of faded jeans. "Happy birthday," I said. "I was so angry at Micah, I left your present at home."

"You can change and get dried off in the bathroom," she said.

In the bathroom, I slipped off my muddy sandals. I washed them in the sink. Then I pushed back my sopping-wet hair and tried to scrape the mud off my face.

I was reaching for a towel when I knocked something on to the floor. I dried my face and looked down.

A load of magazines.

I bent down to pick them up.

I didn't realize what an important moment this was. I didn't realize my life was about to change.

One of the magazines had fallen open. I picked it up and stared at the page.

Stared at an ad. A strange ad. Just a small box with an address inside it.

And the words: REVENGE R US.

Revenge. My favourite word.

I tore out the ad and stuffed it into my pocket. Then I finished getting dressed and hurried downstairs to enjoy the party.

That night when I got home, I threw the ad on to my dressing-table. Then I pulled my diary out of its secret hiding-place—under my mattress.

I wrote in my diary almost every day. I skimmed over what I'd written in the last few weeks.

There were a couple of pages about going bowling with my friend Carl, and a few lines about how I thought Steve Wilson was quite cute. But for most of the summer, my diary was filled with the mean things Micah did to me.

I hope he goes away to college next year—far, far away, I wrote. *Do they have colleges on Mars?*

A few days later, the rainstorms had passed, and we had a blistering heatwave. Carl and I headed for the town pool. We planned to stay underwater until autumn!

Carl and I were in the middle of a cannon-ball contest when the lifeguard blew her whistle. Over the loudspeaker, the pool manager announced, "Adult Swim."

Lots of groans rose up from the pool. That meant we all had to climb out while the grown-ups swam laps for half an hour.

"Want to hit the snack bar?" Carl asked.

A load of kids already mobbed the snack bar, begging for anything frozen and wet. "Nah. It's packed," I replied.

We settled on our towels on the grass. Julie Wilson lounged near by, posing in her bikini. Her brother Steve sat next to her, twirling a Frisbee on one finger.

The loudspeaker clicked on and whistled. We heard a throat being cleared.

"Attention, please," a voice boomed. Not the pool manager's voice. But a very familiar voice.

"More stupid announcements," Steve grumbled.

"Now, for your listening pleasure!" the loud-speaker voice announced cheerily. "Riverdale Swim Club presents a new reading series. To entertain you young people during Adult Swim."

"Huh?" Carl made a face. "They've never done this before."

"Today," the voice boomed, "we present *The Diary of Wade Brill*."

I gasped. Everyone turned to stare at me.

And suddenly I knew whose voice it was.

Micah's!

"No!" I cried. "He wouldn't!"

But he *would*.

"Most of you know Wade," Micah's voice boomed over the speaker. "But in case you don't, she's that skinny girl on the grass with short brownish-blonde hair, wearing the blue bathing-suit that doesn't quite fit."

Kids were murmuring and laughing. A tall boy pointed in my direction. Everybody was staring at me.

I wanted to die.

Micah cleared his throat again. "Episode One: 'Thursday, June twenty-sixth. We went to the supermarket with Mum today. Mum was picking out deodorant when Steve Wilson came down our aisle. He'd just had his hair cut all short and spiky. He looked really cute. I think I'm getting a crush on him.'"

My cheeks flushed hot with anger and embarrassment. How did Micah find it? How did he find my diary?

Everyone at the pool was staring at me. I could feel their eyes burning through me.

I didn't dare look at Steve. But I could hear him laughing, along with the others.

14

I jumped to my feet and raced to the pool office. If only I could stop Micah before he read any more!

"Oh—here's a good one." Micah's voice rose over the pool. "'Saturday, June twenty-eighth. Steve said hi to me today. I mean, he always says hi to me. But today I think he said it in a special way . . .'"

Revenge.

That word stayed in my mind that night and the next day. I knew I couldn't let Micah get away with this. I had waited for twelve years to pay him back.

Now it was time.

I picked up the magazine ad from my dressing-table and read it again and again. REVENGE R US.

What did it mean? Was it a company that got revenge for people? Was that possible?

No phone number. No description. It was so mysterious . . .

The address it gave was on Flamingo Road. That was right on the other side of town, in a very rough, run-down neighbourhood.

I knew I couldn't go there by myself. I needed Carl to come with me. But he was away with his parents for a few days.

I had to wait.

But maybe, I thought, while I'm waiting for Carl

to return, I can work up a little revenge of my own.

I stepped out to the garden to think about it. A hot summer day, sunlight streaming down. Butterflies danced over the flower-beds.

SPLAT! "Got another one!" Mum's voice broke into my thoughts.

I turned and saw her kneeling in the vegetable garden, whacking big silvery slugs with a spade. They splattered in the dirt. She threw their corpses into a bucket.

"Mum, that is so disgusting," I murmured, shaking my head.

"After heavy rains, the slugs all come up," Mum reported. "I'm getting pretty good at flattening them."

SPLAT! "Gotcha!"

"Oh, yuck," I moaned. "I'm going back inside."

"Your brother is in there," Mum said, "with that girl he likes. Sophie Russell."

"She's too good for that creep!" I growled.

Mum looked up from her slugs. "Wade, why are you always picking on Micah?"

"Huh? Me?" I let out a furious shriek, spun round and stormed into the house.

Micah was in the kitchen, trying to impress Sophie. I stood in the hall and spied on them for a while. Micah was spooning coffee into the coffee-maker.

"Want some?" he asked Sophie. "I'm a caffeine freak. I've got to have my three cups a day."

I had to cover my nose so he wouldn't hear me snort with laughter. Three cups a day? He *never* drinks coffee! What a phony!

"I'll have half a cup," Sophie said. "With lots of milk."

This is so sickening, I thought.

I wanted to go screaming to my room. But something told me to stick around.

I was beginning to get an idea. A really mean idea.

Revenge at last . . .

WHACK! I could still hear Mum killing slugs outside. That's what gave me my idea.

I stepped into the kitchen and greeted the two of them. "What are you doing?" I asked innocently. "Making coffee?"

Micah glared at me. His eyes said don't blow this for me, Wade, or you're dead.

I grinned back at him like an adorable little sister. Don't worry, I signalled. I'll play along.

Micah drummed his fingers on the worktop. "I wish this coffee would hurry up and brew. I'm about to freak out here."

"Micah drinks tonnes of coffee," I lied, smiling sweetly at Sophie. Micah looked pleased but suspicious.

"Hey, why don't you two go in the living-room and watch TV?" I suggested. "When the coffee is ready, I'll bring it in to you."

Sophie smiled at Wade. "She's so nice! Not like *my* little sister."

"Yeah." I could tell that Micah was wondering what I was up to. But he said, "Thanks, Wade. Can you bring out some biscuits with that?"

Biscuits? No problem. And a special surprise too.

I watched them head for the living-room. Micah stopped at the mirror to check his hair. His long, wavy dark hair is all he cares about. Except for torturing me.

"I know a man who said he could get me on MTV," he was telling Sophie.

Micah, spelled L-I-A-R.

I crept out to the garden. Mum was so busy whacking slugs she didn't even notice me.

I reached into the slug bucket and scooped out four or five fat, juicy ones.

Yuck.

The wet, slimy things stuck to my hands.

I darted back into the kitchen and dropped the slugs into a coffee cup. Then I washed my hands three times, trying to get the slimy feeling off.

The coffee was finally ready. I poured it into two cups, one with slugs and one without. Then I added plenty of milk and sugar, and stirred. I carried them into the living-room.

Now let's see how much you like coffee, Micah! I sniggered to myself.

Sophie and Micah sat on the sofa. He was running his hand back through his hair and bragging about what a great car he was going to buy.

I handed Sophie the plain coffee. I gave Micah the coffee with the extra added slug treats.

"Thanks, kid," Micah said without even looking at me.

I hung back by the doorway to watch. Sophie sipped her coffee.

Go ahead, Micah, I urged silently. *Drink it . . . drink it . . .*

"So, like, as soon as I have enough money, I want to buy an old Mustang," Micah was saying.

Sophie nodded. "Those cars are really cool."

Drink it. Please—drink it! I urged, my eyes on the cup.

Finally, Micah reached for the coffee cup.

I held my breath.

Go ahead, Micah. Take a biiig sip.

Revenge time at last.

He raised the cup halfway to his lips. Sophie took another sip of her coffee.

I didn't move. Or blink. Or breathe.

Micah lifted the cup higher.

And Mum burst into the room. Coughing. Holding her throat.

"Mum—?" I cried.

"Something caught in my throat," she choked out. "Give me that."

She grabbed the cup from Micah's hand. And took a long sip.

I gasped and slapped both hands against the sides of my face.

"There. That's better," Mum said. "I ate some crisps and . . ." She took another swallow of Micah's coffee.

And her expression changed.

Micah and Sophie both cried out when they saw the slug slide between Mum's lips.

Mum uttered a startled groan. Her mouth twitched.

The slug dropped on to her chin.

Her face twisted in disgust. She plucked the slug off her face between two fingers, and stared at it in shock.

Then I saw her eyes travel to the cup. Another slug flopped over the brim.

Mum let out a choked sound. The cup fell from her hand on to the carpet.

"Wade made the coffee!" Micah declared. He turned to me accusingly.

Mum stared at me, open-mouthed.

"I—I don't believe it!" Micah sputtered. "Wade tried to poison me! She put slugs in the cup!"

Mum's expression changed to anger. Her normally pale face darkened to purple. "Wade—!" she growled. "This is serious. You have *got* to stop picking on your brother!"

I had no choice. I had to get to REVENGE R US. As soon as possible.

Carl got home the next afternoon. I called him and told him the whole story. He didn't want to come with me to the other side of town. But I didn't give him a choice.

After dinner, I waited for him on the front steps. It was a hot, sticky night, the air heavy and damp. A pale sliver of a moon hung low over the trees.

I'd pulled my bike into the driveway so I'd be all ready to go when Carl arrived.

22

The front door opened behind me. Micah and Sophie stepped out. Sophie had stayed for dinner. Micah was rattling Dad's car keys. "I'll give you a lift home," he said. "If you don't mind riding in the Dad-mobile."

Sophie laughed and said she didn't mind. They stepped past me as if I didn't exist. I watched them climb into the car.

"REVENGE R US," I muttered to myself. "You won't be smiling like that in a little while, Micah."

He started the car. The radio blared. He backed down the driveway.

"Nooo!" I jumped up. "Micah—stop!" I screamed.

I suppose he couldn't hear me over the radio. I stared in horror as he backed over my bike!

I held my ears against the horrible crunch of metal.

"Micah! Stop! Stop!" I screamed.

He roared away.

My heart pounding, I hurtled to my bike. Mangled. Bent like a pretzel.

"The last straw," I told myself. "The last straw."

A minute later, Carl showed up on his bike. He has a round face, puffy red cheeks, and short blond hair. He pulled off his glasses, cleaned them on the front of his T-shirt, then slid them back on.

"Is that your bike?" he asked, pointing.

I nodded.

"Micah?" he asked.

I nodded again.

"Let's go," I murmured.

I borrowed Mum's bike from the garage, and we set off.

"Where is this place?" Carl asked.

"Flamingo Road," I said, shifting gears as we headed up a hill.

"Have you ever been to Flamingo Road?" Carl asked.

"No. But I looked on a map. It's over by the railway line."

"Yeah. In Rickoy Flats. The trailer park."

"So?"

"So?" Carl echoed. "It's not the greatest part of town."

"You're not afraid—are you?" I teased.

I expected him to say no, of course not. But instead, he replied, "Yeah. A little."

"Me too," I confessed.

We pedalled through town. The air was so hot and still. It was hard to breathe. Sweat made my T-shirt stick to my back.

Fewer cars passed us on the other side of town. The houses grew smaller and closer together.

We passed a row of deserted apartment buildings. Then an empty plot, cluttered with rubbish.

The road curved and became a gravel path. Our tyres crunched noisily over the gravel.

"Are we going the right way?" Carl asked.

"I . . . think so," I replied. I brushed back my fringe. It was damp from sweat.

Two scrawny dogs were pulling something from an overturned dustbin. I heard the wail of a police siren far in the distance.

The street-lamps suddenly ended. We pedalled over the gravel path into the darkness.

I heard the squeal of car tyres behind us. The thud of shoes over concrete, people running fast.

An animal howled somewhere near by, a long, mournful howl. Inside one of the low, dark buildings, a man laughed.

"I—I don't like this," I stammered.

"Are you sure we're going the right way?" Carl asked in a tiny voice.

I swallowed hard. "I'm not sure."

I braked and lowered my feet to the ground. We had stopped beside a high metal fence.

A sour smell invaded my nose. Fish cooking. Rubbish. Rotten eggs . . .

"Can you read that sign?" Carl squinted through his glasses at a metal sign on the fence.

I moved closer. "Rickey Flats. This is it."

We climbed off our bikes and walked them along the high fence until we found a gate. The metal gate creaked as I pushed it open.

We entered the trailer park, row after row of run-down, ramshackle trailers and mobile homes.

Each trailer had a tiny garden of brown patchy grass. Some of the gardens were filled with junk—a rusty car, stacks of boxes, plaster garden gnomes.

Lights were on in many of the trailers. I heard a baby crying. I smelled food cooking. I heard a woman screaming, screaming at the top of her lungs in a language I couldn't understand.

We walked our bikes slowly through the park until we found Flamingo Road.

Carl nodded towards an old woman sitting on the little porch of her trailer. She grinned at us and waved. "Want to buy a rooster?" she called.

"No, thanks," I called back, surprised at my weak and trembling voice.

I'm scared, I realized.

We shouldn't have come here at night.

Maybe we shouldn't have come here at all.

A chill ran down my back.

At last we came to number 45.

Red and green Christmas lights flickered over the trailer, even though it was July. In the blinking lights, I could see that the trailer was painted bright purple.

Carl turned to me, blinking behind his glasses. His face went red, green, red, green in the flickering lights. "Are you sure you want to do this?" he asked.

I hesitated.

It would be so easy to turn round and go home.

Then I pictured Micah, prowling through my room, stealing my things, stealing my diary. Micah, backing the car over my bike. Micah, ruining my life every day in every way.

Micah, spelled E-N-E-M-Y.

"I'm sure," I told Carl.

We parked our bikes and knocked on the door.

We waited a few seconds.

Then, from inside the trailer, came a terrifying, inhuman cry.

I grabbed Carl's hand.

Aaaahhh! Another horrible cry.

"What was that?" I whispered.

Carl wiped a bead of sweat from his forehead. "Someone screaming?"

The door swung open. A small woman dressed in purple appeared. She had long, stringy black hair that fell over her shoulders. She wore black lipstick, which made her lips pop out from her pale face.

A black crow perched on her shoulder.

"*Aaahhh!*" the crow screeched.

Why was it crying out like that? Was the bird trying to warn us away?

Calm down, Wade, I scolded myself. Don't get carried away. It's just a bird.

Was it just a bird? Why did it keep its round black eyes locked on me that way?

"Come in," the woman said softly. She stepped back to allow Carl and me to enter.

She led us into a small, dark room. I glanced back as she shut the door behind us.

Now we're *trapped* in here, I thought.

I took a deep breath and held it. Calm down, Wade. Calm down.

"I usually don't get visitors this late," the woman said. Her black-lipsticked lips formed a smile. "Did you see my ad?"

I nodded and cleared my throat. "Yes. I—"

The woman clapped her hands. "Customers! Great! Sit down."

We settled in the living-room area, on chairs covered in a purple fabric. A small TV stood against the wall, and a large birdcage dangled above it.

On a chest beside the TV, I spotted a skull. A human skull.

My mouth dropped open. "Is that real?"

Her smile didn't fade. "Probably."

She pulled the crow off her shoulder and petted it. Her black eyes glittered like dark coals in her pale, pale face.

"My name is Iris," she said, stroking the crow's back. "And this is Maggie."

Carl and I introduced ourselves.

"Say hello, Maggie," Iris instructed.

Maggie tilted its head to one side and stared coldly at us.

"Oh, well," Iris sighed. "Maggie's being a bad girl today, aren't you?"

29

The crow fluttered its wings.

A chill ran down my back. Something about the crow seemed so *human*, so *evil*. I glanced at Carl. Could he see that too?

"You both desire revenge?" Iris asked, stroking the crow.

"No," I replied. "Only me."

Iris's eyes lit up. "Revenge against your parents?"

"Huh? No. My brother," I said.

Iris set the crow down on the table. She leaned closer. Her eyes burned into mine. "Tell me why you need help."

I told her about Micah and all the horrible things he had done to me. I was so nervous, my voice shook and I forgot some of the things on my list. Luckily, Carl chimed in with the ones I forgot.

When I finished, Iris gazed at me for a long while. "What kind of revenge do you seek?" she asked finally.

I stared back at her. The bird made soft *CAW-ING* sounds, clicking its beak.

This isn't real, I thought. This is a joke. Some kind of gag. Iris is a phony. She can't be real.

"Can you really get revenge for people?" I blurted out.

She nodded solemnly. Her eyes never left mine. "Maggie and I have some powers," she replied in a whisper.

Her words sent another chill down my back.

Is she evil? I wondered. Have I made a horrible mistake?

"Her brother is always embarrassing her," Carl began to answer the woman's question. "Wade wants to embarrass him back."

"More than that," I said. "I want to humiliate him. I want to *destroy* him. I want to make him feel like a worm. I want to teach him a lesson so that he'll never be nasty to me again."

I took a breath. "He'll be in twelfth grade this autumn," I continued. "I want to really *ruin* his senior year."

"Mmm-hmm." Iris rubbed her chin with long black-fingernailed fingers.

Carl shifted in his chair nervously, twitching his foot.

Iris spoke. "What are you willing to pay for this revenge?"

"Pay?" I asked.

"Yes," Iris said. "If I get your revenge, what will you give me in return?"

I shuddered.

I suddenly realized what this was all about.

I'd seen films about this. And I'd read stories. Horror stories.

"You—you collect *souls*, don't you!" I stammered. "You'll grant me a wish—in exchange for my soul!"

31

Iris threw back her head and laughed. "You've been watching too much TV," she said. "I don't know anything about souls. I'm trying to start a business here. If I got paid in souls, I'd starve to death!"

I stared at her blankly. I was so confused, I could hardly think straight.

Carl leaned over and whispered, "Wade, I think she's talking about money."

"Money?" I cried. "But I don't *have* any money."

Iris rolled her eyes. She picked up the crow again. "Just my luck, Maggie. I finally get a customer, and she has no money. What are we going to do?"

She sighed. "Well, I'll tell you what, Wade. I'll give you a free trial."

"Thank you!" I cried.

Iris narrowed her eyes. "Maybe later, I'll think of something you can do to repay me."

"Like what?" I asked, feeling my throat tighten.

She shook her head. "Later. I'll think of something."

She brushed her long black hair behind her shoulders. "Do we have a deal?"

I swallowed hard. "I . . . I suppose so."

Iris reached over and shook hands with me. Her long black fingernails scraped my palm. Her hand was soft and damp.

"So . . . revenge against your brother, Micah," she said, shutting her eyes. "Let me think . . .

"Aha. I have a very good idea. Just the thing."

Moving her lips silently, she rubbed the crow's back, once, twice . . . three times.

Her eyes shot open. "There. It is done."

"Huh? What did you do?" I demanded.

"A lovely little revenge. Your brother will have a terrible accident—and he'll never recover."

"Nooooo!" I wailed. "No! No—*please*! That's too much! That's not what I want! Take it back! Take it back!"

"Sorry," Iris said coldly. "It's too late."

"That's *horrible*!" Carl cried.

I jumped to my feet. "Take it back!" I shrieked at Iris. "You can't do that to Micah! Take it back—now!"

I tore at my hair with both hands. I let out a frantic scream. "What have I done? Oh, no! What have I done?"

Iris shook her head. Her hair fell over her face. "Once a spell is cast, I'm afraid—"

She pushed back her head. Her mouth opened in a wide O. "Oh. Wait. Hold your horses. I forgot something! I left out a step."

I let out a long sigh. "You mean—the spell didn't work?"

"No," Iris replied. "I left something out. It's *your* revenge. That means you also have to rub Maggie's back three times."

"So Micah is okay?" I demanded. "There's not going to be an accident?"

"Accident? No. Not unless you wish for it."

Iris held Maggie out on her arm. "There are so many rules to using this crow," she said. "So many rules. Here. You think of your revenge. Then you rub Maggie's back three times—and it will come true."

"Thank goodness," I breathed. I wanted to make Micah suffer. But I didn't want him to really be hurt.

"Come on," Iris urged. "Choose your revenge. I don't have all day."

Carl and I huddled round the crow. "What should we do?" I asked Carl. "It has to be bad, but not *that* bad."

Carl scrunched up his face and thought hard. He began to scratch his neck.

"Why are you scratching like that?" I asked.

He made a face at me. "I have an itch."

"That's what we'll do!" Iris declared. "That's perfect!"

"Huh?" Carl and I both gaped at her.

"We'll give your brother an itch," Iris said, her dark eyes flashing excitedly.

I shook my head. "An itch? What kind of revenge is that?"

Iris leaned towards me. "An itch that won't go away," she said softly. "An itch that gets worse the more you scratch it. An itch that spreads and spreads—until his whole body itches. His teeth itch. His eyeballs itch. His tongue itches. And he can't stop it!"

"Well . . ." I hesitated.

"He won't be able to do anything," Iris continued excitedly. "He won't be able to go anywhere. He'll just stay home scratching . . . scratching and scratching until he scratches all his skin off!"

"Sounds good," I said.

"Cool," Carl agreed.

Iris held the crow in one hand. She shut her eyes. She rubbed Maggie's back three times.

"Now you do it," she said. She held the bird out to me.

I started to reach for Maggie. But I stopped myself. "Is this really free?" I asked.

Iris frowned. "Don't worry about it."

What did that mean? Was this some kind of a trick?

I didn't care. I wanted my revenge against Micah.

I closed my eyes and made my wish. Then I rubbed the crow once, twice . . . three times.

Carl and I pedalled our bikes home as fast as we could. I burst breathlessly into the den, looking for Micah. Dad sat in an armchair, reading a mystery novel.

"Wade, where have you been?" he demanded, closing the book.

"I—I borrowed Mum's bike," I stammered, struggling to catch my breath. "Carl and I—we went for a long bike ride."

Dad narrowed his eyes at me. "On your mum's bike? What happened to *your* bike?"

"Micah ran over it!" I exclaimed. "He backed the car over it. It's completely wrecked!"

Dad *tsk-tsked* and shook his head. I expected him to say, "Micah will have to be punished for that."

But instead, he murmured, "I'm sure it was an accident. You shouldn't leave your bike in the driveway, Wade."

"*Aaaagggh!*" I wanted to strangle Dad.

But Mum came striding into the room. "There you are!" she declared, smiling at me. "Dessert time, everyone! Who wants dessert? We all ran out after dinner without any dessert."

Micah came clomping down the stairs. All four of us made our way into the dining-room. Mum sliced a chocolate cake she had bought. Dad scooped out vanilla ice-cream to go with it.

"Did you know you backed over my bike?" I asked Micah angrily.

Micah grabbed the scoop from Dad's hand and scooped himself two extra helpings of ice-cream. "That piece of junk?" he replied. "I hope it didn't ruin the tyres."

"Can we have some pleasant conversation for a change?" Mum asked. She glared at me. Then she smiled at Micah. "It's such a rare treat to have you home one evening."

"Yeah," I muttered. "He's always out getting into trouble with his geek friends."

"At least I *have* friends!" Micah shot back.

"Please. Give us a break, Wade," Mum groaned.

Me? Why does she only criticize me?

Micah started talking about the Mustang he wanted to buy. He begged Mum and Dad for the hundredth time to lend him the money so he could have the car for the summer.

I didn't hear their reply. I tuned them all out.

I watched Micah. And waited.

Waited for the itching to start. Waited for him to start scratching . . . scratching . . . scratching until he squirmed and twisted in agony, ripping all his skin off.

He shoved the last piece of cake into his mouth. Then he burped really loudly.

Mum and Dad laughed. They just think everything he does is adorable.

Start itching, I silently urged. *Come on, Micah. Start itching.*

He drummed his fingers impatiently while the rest of us finished our dessert. He seemed very restless.

But itchy? No.

I kept my eyes on him. I didn't want to miss it when it started. I wanted to see every moment of my revenge.

"More ice-cream, anyone?" Dad asked, waving the scoop.

Micah picked up his fork.

He's going to start scratching himself with it, I knew.

Here it comes. The Big Itch has started.

No. Micah tapped the fork on the tabletop. Then he reached across the table and started tapping it on my head.

"Get off!" I cried. I shoved his hand away.

He spiked the fork into my chocolate cake and snagged a chunk of my icing. He popped the icing into his mouth.

39

Mum and Dad laughed again.

I didn't care. I knew that I'd be the one laughing—very soon.

But when? When?

Why hadn't the itch started?

Finally, I couldn't take it any more. "Micah," I asked, "do you feel strange or anything?"

"Not as strange as you look!" he shot back. He snatched the last chunk of icing off my plate. Then he hurried back up to his room.

I should have asked Iris how long the spell takes, I decided.

I clicked off my bedside lamp and slid under the covers. Silvery moonlight lit up the curtains. Shadows of trees danced over the bedroom walls.

Micah will probably start itching in the morning, I told myself. Iris probably made the spell start tomorrow.

I yawned. My legs ached from the long bike ride. I fell asleep quickly. A deep, dreamless sleep.

The room was still dark when I awoke. I squinted at the clock radio. Five-fifteen in the morning.

What woke me up?

My back tingled. Sort of a stinging sensation.

I reached my hand to scratch it. But the tingling was just out of my reach.

40

I rubbed my back against the mattress. It didn't seem to help.

The skin prickled and burned. The tingling spread quickly.

I reached back and scratched with both hands.

My whole back was tingling now.

No. Not tingling.

Itching.

I sat up and rubbed my back against the wooden headboard.

I scratched my shoulders.

"Oh, nooooo," I moaned. "Oh, noooo."

I'm itching—and it's spreading fast!

I rubbed my sides. My arms. My knees.

I tried not to scratch. But rubbing didn't help.

"Ohhhhh." Moaning in agony, I couldn't stop myself. I started to scratch.

At first, I scratched lightly. But it didn't help. My skin prickled. I scratched harder.

Chills swept up and down my body. I was shaking and shivering.

And scratching myself furiously like a dog with fleas.

"Hellllp," I murmured. "I need . . . help."

I staggered to the bathroom and slammed the door behind me.

The back of my neck throbbed and itched. It felt as if a thousand insects were crawling round and round my body, covering my skin, pinching me, biting me.

I started pawing frantically through the medicine cabinet. There must be some kind of itch stopper in here, I thought.

I found some pink lotion for poison ivy. With trembling hands, I slathered it over my shoulders, my arms.

Please work, I prayed. Please ...

I clawed at my legs. My toes itched. My knees itched.

The pink stuff didn't help at all. Now I was itchy *and* sticky!

Maybe a hot bath, I decided.

I ran water in the tub and took off my night-shirt. I twisted and squirmed, struggling to scratch my back, my shoulder-blades. And now my *teeth* started to tingle and itch!

I soaked in the tub, letting the hot water rise over me.

Please ... please ...

No. Not helping.

The insides of my ears itched!

My eyes itched. I rubbed them, rubbed them until my eyelids burned.

Out of the tub. My whole body shaking.

My teeth chattering.

Got to get help. Got to go back to Iris.

I stumbled back to my room. Bent to scratch my legs.

Oh, no. Thin rivers of bright-red blood trickled down my legs. I was scratching the skin off!

Tell Mum and Dad? No. They'd never believe me. They couldn't help.

Just get back to Iris.

Shaking violently, struggling not to scratch, I pulled on jeans and a top. My whole body throbbed. As if thousands and thousands of insects were swarming on my skin.

Not quite six in the morning yet. Still grey outside. I didn't care. I grabbed the phone. Punched in Carl's number.

He answered sleepily on the fourth ring. "Hello?" His voice choked with sleep.

"Mwwwwammmmm," I uttered.

Oh, no! No! This can't be happening!

"Who is this?" Carl demanded angrily.

"Mwwwww!" I moaned. "Mwwwammmmm."

"Whoever you are, you're not funny!" Carl bellowed. "You woke me up!"

"Mwwwwwww?" I cried.

The line went dead.

"Mwwwwwumm."

I can't talk. I realized. My tongue—it itches so badly. Stinging and prickling. It feels as if it's fallen asleep. My tongue won't *move*!

My whole body feels as if it's asleep.

I can't take it!

Ow! Ow! Ow!

My legs wobbled. I scratched my neck. The skin was all raw and sore.

I brushed my hair furiously, trying to stop my *hair* from itching. My scalp . . . my ears . . .

Could I pedal Mum's bike across town to Iris's trailer?

44

Maybe if I ride really fast, I won't notice the itching so much, I decided.

I finished getting dressed. I practically screamed when I had to slide my throbbing feet into trainers.

My skin ... my skin ... burning ... burning ...

I had no choice. I had to try.

But could I find Iris again in that maze of trailers and mobile homes? What was the address?

The magazine ad. The address is on the ad.

Scratching my shoulder, I frantically searched the top of my dressing-table. Not there.

Where? Where is the ad?

My jeans pocket. My hands ached and stung as I searched the pockets.

Not there.

Where was the ad? Where was it?

How would I ever find her?

I had no choice. I had to get to Iris—fast.

I couldn't talk. I could barely walk.

My whole body itched. Itched so hard it hurt.

I gasped for air. The pain—everywhere, everywhere—was making it hard to breathe. Even the inside of my nose itched!

Forget the address, I decided. I'll find the trailer. I *have* to find it!

I stumbled out of the house and grabbed Mum's bike from the garage. Could I ride it? My hands were shaking. My whole body shook. Chill after chill swept down my back.

Panting hard, I pulled myself on to the seat and forced my legs to pedal. Leaning forward, I gripped the handlebars as tightly as I could.

I wanted to scratch and scratch and scratch. Gripping the handlebars kept me from clawing all my skin off!

The morning sun still hadn't risen. Low, heavy clouds darkened the sky.

I rode through the thick grey air. Past town, the shops empty and dark. Along the railway line towards the trailer park.

Grey . . . everything so foggy and grey. As if I were pedalling through a misty dream.

I found the trailer park and slowed my bike, riding along the high metal fence.

My back itched. My stomach itched. My arms and legs tingled and throbbed.

Wade, don't scratch! I ordered myself.

My hands were shaking so hard, I had to lean my shoulder against the gate to push it open. I left my bike beside the gate and began trotting along the rows of trailers. As I ran, I shoved my hands into my jeans pockets to keep from scratching.

Where is it? Where is Iris's trailer?

Thunder rumbled in the distance. The storm clouds gathered over me. The park was as dark as night.

A dog barked somewhere near by. A light flickered on in a rusted trailer ahead of me. A man peeked out, then quickly pulled the curtain closed.

Trailer after trailer, all dark, all grey.

The whole world grey and growing darker. I felt a cold splash of rain on my itching forehead.

I turned and trotted along another row.

Whoa. I stopped.

Have I been here already? Why do these trailers look familiar?

I spun round. Yes. I'd already searched this row. But which way had I come?

I spun round again. Where was the front fence? Where was the gate?

I'm lost, I realized.

I've lost all sense of direction.

I looked down—and saw that I was scratching my arms—scratching as hard as I could, *without even realizing it*!

I forced my hands back into my jeans pockets. Then I started jogging again, my eyes searching up and down the long rows of trailers and mobile homes.

I can't find it, I realized. *I'm really lost.*

My eyeballs were itching now. The itching made them water. Tears ran down my tingling, burning face. I could barely see.

I stopped. Breathing hard, I leaned against the wall of a mobile home.

And heard a *CAAAW CAAAAW*.

Maggie! Yes! Running frantically, I followed the sound of the crow.

I let out a happy cry as the purple trailer came into view. No lights were on. But I didn't care. I lurched up to the door and pounded as hard as I could with both fists.

The door finally swung open, and I fell inside.

"Huh?" Iris uttered a startled gasp. She stood

48

over me in a baggy purple robe. Her black hair fell in tangles over her shoulders. "What are *you* doing here?" she demanded.

"Mwwwaaaamm!" I replied.

My tongue—it itched so hard, it wouldn't move. The roof of my mouth itched too!

"Muuwwwwwm. Muhhhhm?"

Iris gaped at me. She raised her hands to her cheeks. Her black fingernails tapped her face.

"Maaawwwwm!" I screeched.

I couldn't help myself. I had to scratch. Frantically, I scratched my neck. The back of my arms.

Scratching . . . scratching like an animal.

"Oh, no!" Iris cried. She grabbed my hands and pulled them towards her. "You're itching—aren't you!"

I nodded. "Mwwwwwum."

"My spell!" she exclaimed. "I did something wrong!" She slapped her forehead.

"Mwwwwum maaawwm!" I cried, gesturing wildly.

"I can't!" she declared, still gripping my hands. "I can't stop it! I only know how to start it! I don't know how to stop it!"

I sank to my knees. My body itched so horribly. I was shaking. My teeth chattered. My whole body vibrated.

Across the room, the crow cawed loudly in its cage.

Gasping, struggling to breathe, I raised my

arm and pointed to the cage. "Mwaaaam! Maaawwm?"

Iris squinted at me. Then she turned to the bird.

"Maybe if I cast another spell, it will stop the first one!" she declared. "If I cast an *opposite* spell . . ."

"Maaaww!" I screamed frantically. I pushed her with both hands towards the birdcage.

Hurry! I thought. *Please—try it! Try it! Hurry!*

I stood trembling, my whole body burning, as she reached into the cage. She pulled Maggie out with one hand.

She held the crow up to her face and spoke in a whisper. "Soft, smooth skin. Give Wade soft, smooth skin."

Iris rubbed the crow's back three times.

Then she shoved the bird towards me. "Quick, Wade—rub Maggie's back."

My hand shook so hard, I nearly knocked the bird out of Iris's hand. Finally, I managed to raise my hand over the crow's back, and I rubbed it once, twice . . . three times.

My body itching, throbbing in pain, I stared at the crow. And waited.

Waited for the change.

Waited . . . waited . . .

Nothing happened.

Iris stood watching me, studying me, her arms crossed tightly in front of her purple robe.

"It didn't work!" I cried.

And then I gasped. I was *talking*!

"Hey—!" I exclaimed. "My tongue—it's stopped itching!"

I rubbed my arms. They felt smooth and soft. I ran my hands through my hair. It didn't itch any longer.

"Oh, wow!" I cried. I dropped on to her sofa. It felt so good to feel *nothing*!

"Whew." Iris let out a long sigh of relief. "Glad that's over," she murmured, shaking her head.

Outside the front window, a jagged bolt of lightning flashed across the grey sky.

"Over?" I said.

She brushed her long hair off her face. "Sorry it didn't work out." She shrugged. "I suppose you get what you pay for."

"But you owe me a revenge!" I insisted.

She scowled. "Owe you? You didn't pay me anything. How can I owe you?"

"You promised me a revenge!" I declared, jumping to my feet. My nice, smooth, not-itching feet. "You promised me! And instead—instead—!"

"Okay, okay. Calm down." She gestured with both hands for me to sit back down on the sofa.

But I followed her to the tiny stove where she poured water into a silvery kettle. "You owe me," I repeated.

"Okay, okay." She dropped the kettle on to the burner. "We'll try again. But I can't keep doing these things for free. I'm going to have to collect someday."

I wasn't listening to her. I was thinking hard about what kind of revenge I wanted for my brother.

Something bad, I knew. Something worse than itching.

Itching . . . itching . . . I had suffered because of Micah. So *what* if he didn't know about it!

"What does Micah care about more than anything?" I asked myself aloud.

Torturing me?

Buying a car?

That girl Sophie?

His hair?

Yes! His hair! Sophie and his hair!

"Micah has a date with this girl Sophie tomorrow night," I told Iris. "He really wants to impress her. Before he sees her, he tries on all the clothes he owns. He spends hours on his hair! He buys more hair spray and gel and goo than my mum!"

Iris turned from the stove. "His hair, huh?" She stroked Maggie. "Then why don't we do something to his hair? In front of Sophie?"

"I like it!" I exclaimed. "We could make it fall out. You know. A clump at a time—until he's bald!"

Iris chuckled. "Yes. It will have to fall out slowly. Then, by the end of the evening he'll be completely bald!"

"Yes! Yes! Let's do it!" I declared.

Iris narrowed her dark eyes at me. "You're sure?"

"Yes!"

"This will be your last free revenge—understand?"

"Yes!" I agreed. "Just do it!"

She closed her eyes and rubbed Maggie three times.

"Your turn," she said.

I shut my eyes and imagined Micah sitting with Sophie at the Burger Barn. And I pictured Micah's hair all over the table, all over their burgers, all over his lap.

Giggling to myself, I rubbed my hands over Maggie's feathery back.

"This is perfect," I sighed. "Revenge at last!"

The next night, I watched Micah get ready to go out with Sophie. "Those jeans are far too long on you," I told him. "They're dragging over your shoes."

"So?" he replied nastily. "That's the way I like them." He shook his head, sneering at me. "You really are a moron."

He turned back to the bathroom mirror and studied his hair. I sat on the edge of the tub and watched him.

"Get lost," he snarled. "If I wanted an audience, I'd charge admission."

"I won't bother you," I chirped.

I don't have to bother you, I thought, smiling to myself. Iris is going to bother you for me— big time!

Micah combed his wavy dark hair forward. It reached below his chin.

Then he carefully combed it straight back, working till every hair was in place.

He stared in the mirror, admiring himself. Then he set the comb on the sink.

I couldn't help checking it for loose hairs. A few strands were stuck in the comb. Not more than usual, but a few.

A warm, happy feeling washed over me. Those strands of hair were the beginning of a long, long night for Micah.

He rubbed gel in his hands and started fluffing his hair with it.

I giggled.

"What are you laughing at, Jerk Face?" Micah demanded.

"Nothing," I said innocently.

"My hair frizzes if I don't use gel, okay?" he snapped. "Why don't you go and write in your diary? Everybody at the pool has been begging me for the next instalment!"

My face burned. But I swallowed my anger. I'll get my revenge soon enough, I thought.

Micah fluffed his hair some more, then blew it dry. Then he wet it again and combed some kind of gunk through it. Then he blew it dry. Then he fluffed it again.

"I really need a trim," he muttered.

You'll get more than a trim, I thought to myself. A lot more!

"I've got to go," he said at last. "You can sit on the edge of the tub all night. I've got better things to do."

He switched off the bathroom light, even though I was still sitting there. Then he shoved me—shoved me hard, pushing me into the tub.

"Take a bath, Wade. You need one!"

"Hey!" I protested. "You creep!"

I scrambled out of the bath and followed him downstairs. I watched him get into Dad's car and drive away.

Have fun, Micah, I thought. Too bad you didn't bring a hat. Or a paper bag to keep your precious hair in!

I had to laugh. I wondered if I had film in my camera.

I'll wait up and snap his picture when he comes home, I decided. I need a photo of his big, bald head to keep for ever.

I brought my camera downstairs and settled in the den in front of the TV. I felt a little disappointed. I'd hoped Micah's hair would start to fall out *before* he left the house.

It would have made my evening so nice to see the spell begin.

But it was fun thinking of him, out with Sophie. I imagined her touching his hair and pulling a big hunk of it out in her hand.

Maybe she'd scream!

That would be excellent.

I hit the kitchen and microwaved a big bowl of popcorn. Then I returned to the TV.

I was half-watching a show on the Discovery

Channel about the world's cutest penguins. Thinking about Micah as I watched. Stuffing popcorn into my mouth.

It took me a while to realize something was wrong.

I dipped my hand into the popcorn bowl. "Hey—!" The popcorn was sticking to my hand.

"What's going on?"

I lowered my gaze. Stared down at my hand. Stared at it. Stared . . .

And then I opened my mouth in a shrill scream of horror.

I leaped up from the chair. The bowl toppled over, sending an avalanche of popcorn on to the floor.

I didn't care.

I gripped my hand. Plucked popcorn kernels from it. Brought it close to my face, studying it in horror.

"No! This is too weird!" I protested.

Thick black stubble had sprouted on the back of my hand. On *both* hands! Short, like men's whiskers.

I rubbed the hair. It felt stiff and bristly.

I pulled up the sleeve of my shirt.

"Oh, nooooo." I uttered a sick moan. The bristly black hair went all the way up my arms.

"No. Oh, please. No!" I cried.

My heart pounded as I tore across the room to the front hall mirror.

I'm not a werewolf! I told myself. *It's not a full moon.*

My T-shirt collar suddenly made my neck itch. I turned in front of the mirror.

"Oh, noooooo!"

The thick black hair had sprouted over the back of my neck.

Was that a shadow under my chin?

No. More hair growing! Growing all round my neck!

I stared open-mouthed, raising my hands to the mirror. And as I studied myself, the stubby black hair grew. The hair on the backs of my hands was two centimetres long now. Straight and thick as bear fur.

"Aaaack!" I let out another cry as I saw the hair sprout on my forehead.

My stomach lurched. I could feel my dinner coming up.

Tufts of black hair poked out of my ears!

"Iris!" I growled. "Iris strikes again!"

How did she do this? How did she so completely mess up?

The straight black hair slid over my eyes, like a fringe. The hair on my arms pushed out from under my sleeves.

I was wearing denim shorts. I gazed down at my legs—furry gorilla legs!

My hands! My hands looked like *paws*! Furry black animal paws!

The hair is growing, growing so fast! I realized. Staring into the mirror, I no longer looked like me. I no longer looked like a *human*!

"I—I'm some sort of a *creature*!" I cried.

I spun away from the mirror. I couldn't bear to look any more.

"Iris," I muttered. "I've got to get back to Iris."

I started to run. My legs scraped together. "Ohhhh." What a sick feeling. Fur rubbing against fur.

Mum and Dad were sitting out on the back patio, sipping iced tea. "I'm going for a walk!" I called out to them. "Be right back!"

I raced out to the garage before they could see me. I hopped on to Mum's bike and tried to pedal. "OWWWW!"

The thick fur caught in the spokes!

I toppled off the bike. And landed on my furry back.

I can't ride a bike! I realized.

I scrambled to my feet. Fur covered my shoes. I pushed thick fur out of my eyes. And started to lumber on foot to Carl's house.

I was crossing the street to the next block when I heard a dog barking. Distant at first. But then I heard the rapid *THUD* of paws on the grass.

I turned. A big black Lab. Yapping excitedly. It circled me, jaws snapping as it barked.

"Go home!" I ordered it. "Bad dog! Get going! Go home!"

I tried to shoo it away with my furry arms.

But that seemed to get the dog more excited. Yapping loudly, it circled me, circled me.

I tried to run. But my legs were weighed down

by the long fur. My whole body felt as if it weighed a tonne!

Another dog—some kind of terrier—came running after me. It sniffed my leg fur. Then started barking, a shrill, angry cry.

"Go home! Go home! Please!" I wailed.

Two more dogs appeared. Barking excitedly. Circling. Criss-crossing in front of me.

Again, I tried to run.

I counted six dogs now. All acting ferocious, barking and growling.

What were they going to do? Were they about to attack me?

Gripped with panic, I totally lost it. "I'm not an animal!" I screamed at them. "I'm a human! Go home! Go home!"

I could see Carl's house next door.

It seemed ten miles away!

The dogs were growling now. Some of them had their heads lowered, their backs arched, preparing to attack.

They think I'm a bear or something, I realized.

Of *course* they do. I *look* like a bear!

"Go home! Please—go home!" I begged.

The black Lab uttered a high-pitched growl—and jumped.

Its front paws struck my furry shoulders. Its heavy body slammed into me.

With a cry, I fell to the ground—with the Lab on top of me.

"No—stop! Get off! Down! Down!" I shrieked.

I heard howls and snarls all around.

I struggled to scramble to my feet. But a big Alsatian lowered its head—and knocked me back to the grass.

And then, growling and snuffling, the dogs all pounced.

I felt hot breath on my face. Teeth tugged at my fur.

They piled on . . . piled on . . .

And I knew I was dead meat.

Over the growls of the dogs, I heard a high scream.

The dogs heard it too. They stopped barking and growling. A few of them let go of my fur and tilted their heads, listening.

Yellow light slanted over the grass.

"Get away! Get away! Go home! Shoo!" a voice yelled.

The dogs hesitated. They turned towards the light.

"Go home! Go home—now!"

And yes! The whole pack turned away from me—and ran off. Paws thudding heavily on the grass, they ran off in every direction.

Feeling dizzy, my heart pounding, I pulled myself up on one furry elbow. And saw Carl jump off his porch and approach me slowly.

"Whoa," he muttered.

Then I saw the garden rake. He raised it in both hands. Pulled it back to use as a weapon.

I rose to my knees, brushing grass and leaves from my fur.

Carl kept his eyes on me as he walked nearer. The rake was tensed in his hands, ready to swing.

"Easy, boy," he said to me. "Did you escape from the zoo or something?"

I opened my mouth to reply. But choked on the words.

I cleared my throat. Brushed fur from my eyes.

"Easy, boy," Carl urged timidly.

"Stop calling me *boy*," I snapped. "What's wrong with you, Carl? It's me!"

"Huh?" The rake fell from his hands. It landed on his foot. He winced in pain—but didn't take his eyes off me.

"You—you *talk*?" he stammered.

"It's me. Wade!" I declared.

He let out another gasp. I thought his eyes were going to pop out from behind his glasses.

"Wade?"

"Iris did this," I told him, gesturing to my bear fur.

I hoisted myself to my feet. It wasn't easy. The fur had grown even longer. Hunched there in Carl's front garden, I knew I looked like a black mound of hay!

"You—you—you—" Carl could only sputter.

"Iris messed up again," I explained. "She was supposed to make Micah go bald."

"Those dogs—" Carl choked out.

"They thought I was a bear," I said. "Or maybe they thought I was a really big, ugly dog."

"What are we going to do?" Carl cried.

"Guess," I replied sharply. "We're going back to Iris's trailer."

It wasn't easy.

We walked in the darkest shadows. I tried not to let anyone see me.

Dogs followed us, packs of them. Sniffing. Nipping at my fur.

Carl tried to keep them away. But he didn't have much luck.

Just past town, some teenagers in a van started following us. They were calling out the window, laughing and making rude jokes about me.

When Carl told them to mind their own business, they laughed and sped off.

And then we heard police sirens from down the street. "Someone must have reported seeing a weird creature!" I cried. "Hide me! Where can I hide?"

"You're too big to hide," Carl said.

He was right. My long, thick fur made me as big as a grizzly bear!

We saw flashing lights. Two police cars came roaring towards us.

No time to run. No time to hide.

I froze, waiting for them to stop.

Waiting . . . waiting . . .

And the cars sped right past us.

My heart beating in my chest, I watched the flashing lights until the two cars rode out of sight.

"We've got to hurry," I told Carl. "The fur keeps growing. It—it's so heavy now. Soon I won't be able to walk."

We made it to the trailer park in twenty minutes. This time, I remembered where Iris lived.

I was breathing hard, sweating under my heavy coat of fur. I had to keep brushing the thick hair away from my eyes so that I could see.

Carl knocked on the trailer door.

It swung open.

Darkness inside.

"Iris?" I called in. "Iris? Are you home?"

"*Awwwwk!*" Maggie's cry. The only reply.

I leaned into the doorway. "Anybody home?" I tried again.

No answer.

"Let's go in," Carl suggested.

I held back. "We can't go in there if Iris isn't home," I said.

I pulled a fly out of my arm fur. "Yuck. Carl— I think I'm *crawling* with bugs!"

"Come on. Let's go in," he repeated. "We'll use

Maggie. We can get you back to normal—without Iris."

"Maybe . . ." I said softly.

Carl stepped inside the dark trailer. "Come on, Hairy. Nothing to be afraid of."

Nothing?

Then why did I have such a bad feeling about this?

"Oh!" I bumped the sides of the trailer door.

My fur had grown so thick, I looked like a massive Koosh Ball. Too big to squeeze into Iris's trailer.

With a groan, I heaved myself forward—and bumped into the door-frame again. The whole trailer shook.

"Carl—I'm too big. I can't get in!" I cried.

He peered out at me from the dark doorway. "Turn sideways," he instructed. "Try it sideways."

It took all my strength to turn myself round. Then I slid my side towards the door. And squeezed inside.

"*CAAAAAAW!*" Maggie let out a chilling cry, as if warning us away. The sound made my fur stand on end.

"Where's the light?" Carl asked, sounding tense and frightened. "Find a lamp or something."

I bumped into a table. Something heavy fell to the floor with a loud crash.

Carl and I both screamed.

"Calm down! Calm down!" we both cried to each other.

"*CAAAAWAAAAWW!*" Another shrill shriek from Maggie, somewhere in the dark.

"Why does that bird sound so human?" Carl asked softly.

"Iris?" I called. "Iris? Are you in the bedroom?"

No reply.

I bumped into a sofa or a chair. "Ouch!" As I cried out, a deep blackness fell over me. The dark room grew even darker.

"Carl—I can't see!" I cried.

It took me a few seconds to realize that my heavy fur had blanketed my eyes. I brushed it away with both furry paws.

"I—I can't take this much longer," I stammered.

Yellow light washed over the room. Carl had found a table lamp.

"*CAAAAAAAHAAW!*"

Maggie hopped up and down excitedly on a wooden perch in her cage.

"We've got to hurry," I told Carl. My voice was muffled by the thick fur over my face. "I'm so heavy . . . I can barely breathe."

Carl crossed the cluttered room and grabbed

the handle on top of Maggie's cage. The crow cawed and hopped, as if protesting.

"Hurry," I choked out. "I . . . I'm smothering under here."

He set the cage on the table. Opened the door and pulled out the crow. Then he placed the bird in one of my hairy palms.

"Make your wish," Carl instructed. "Rub the bird. You saw how Iris did it. You can do it too."

"I hope so," I murmured softly.

I shut my eyes. My heart pounded as I tried to decide what to wish for.

Go away, I thought. *Hair—go away.*

I rubbed my heavy paw over Maggie's back. Once, twice . . . three times.

I opened my eyes. Maggie tilted her head and stared up at me with one glittering black eye. Studied me coldly, the eye gleaming like a black jewel.

I forced myself to look away. "Nothing is happening," I moaned.

"Give it a little time," Carl urged. He carried the crow back to its cage. He set it on the perch and closed the cage door.

"I haven't got much time," I said in a whisper. "Too heavy . . . I'm too heavy."

My knees were bending. My legs couldn't hold me. I felt as if I were sinking under the mountain of black fur. Sinking to the floor.

"Why isn't it working? Why?" I wailed.

Carl swallowed hard. "Give it time, Wade. It's only been a few seconds."

"Give me the crow again," I ordered him. "I'll try again. I'll try a different wish. I'll try *ten* more wishes!"

Carl didn't reply. He didn't move.

"Carl?" I cried. "What is it?"

I brushed the thick fur from in front of my eyes. Carl had his head lowered. What was he staring at?

"Carl?" I cried. "What are you doing? What's wrong?"

"Uh . . . well . . ." His eyes bulged behind his glasses. Even in the dim lamplight, I could see the horror on his face.

"Wade . . ." he murmured. He raised his hands to me.

"Oh, no!" I gasped.

I stared at the thick black hair sprouting on the backs of Carl's hands.

"It—it's growing," Carl stammered.

He lowered his hands and turned to me angrily. "Why, Wade? Why did you do this to me?"

"I didn't!" I protested. "Something went wrong. Maybe it's that stupid crow! Maybe—"

I didn't have a chance to finish my sentence.

A loud scream from the open door behind us made us both jump.

I struggled to turn round. But I was weighed down by fur. I couldn't move.

"It's Iris!" Carl gasped.

She stormed furiously into the trailer. Her long purple dress swirled behind her. "Who are you? What are you doing in here?" she demanded.

"It's me," I moaned. "Wade."

"We're growing hair!" Carl cried, holding up his hairy hands. "You've got to do something."

Iris's mouth dropped open. She grabbed a clump of my fur in one hand and gave it a tug.

"Ouch!" I cried.

"Oh, my!" Iris murmured. She took a step back, her eyes moving from me to Carl.

"I can't breathe under here," I choked out. "And it's two hundred degrees. Do something!"

"Do something—please!" Carl echoed. He had long fur trailing down the back of his neck. And strands of black fur were lowering from inside his nose.

"I've messed up again," Iris said, shaking her head. "That's the problem with starting up a new business. It takes time to get the bugs out."

"Don't say bugs," I murmured. I knew my fur was crawling with them.

Suddenly, my knees gave out. They couldn't carry the weight any more. I sank to the floor.

"I can't breathe . . ." I moaned. "The hair . . . it's *smothering* me. I can't *see*!"

I heard Iris cross the room. I heard Maggie caw excitedly.

"I'm trying another spell," Iris announced. "I'll try something fast-acting."

"I've already tried something!" I wailed.

Iris gasped. "You shouldn't mess with Maggie, Wade. I'm warning you. It's dangerous. It's not as simple as it looks. There are rules . . ."

"Please," I begged. "Hurry."

Silence for a few moments.

I heard the squeak of the cage door opening. I heard the flutter of Maggie's wings.

More silence. More silence.

And then I began to itch.

Oh, no! I thought. She brought back the itching spell. I'm buried under two tonnes of hair—*and* I'm going to start itching to death!

But no.

The fur pulled up, away from my eyes.

I suddenly felt lighter. I sat up.

My arms itched. My legs itched. My whole body itched.

Because the fur was sliding INTO my skin!

I sat on the floor in stunned amazement. Feeling the hairs slide, slide into me, growing smaller, smaller. As if someone had thrown a hair-growing video into rewind.

A few seconds later, Carl and I stared at each other. Back to normal.

I rubbed my arms. Smooth. I rubbed the back of my neck. Hair-free!

I felt so light. Light as a bird!

Carl pulled me to my feet. We both cheered happily.

Still holding the crow in her palm, Iris shook her head unhappily. "Sorry," she murmured. "I'm so sorry."

"Does this mean Micah didn't go bald tonight?" I demanded.

"I've messed up," Iris sighed. "I owe you one. One more try."

I hesitated. So far, my revenge wasn't exactly

working out. Should I give up the whole idea?

"I think I know what the problem is," Iris said thoughtfully. She set Maggie on to her shoulder. "I think you have to go home. If you're not here, the spell will work on your brother—not on you."

"Okay," I agreed. "I suppose we should try one more time."

It would be a shame, I decided, to go through all this torture and *still* not get revenge on Micah.

"But what are you going to do to him?" I asked.

A strange smile spread over Iris's black lips. "I'm going to make your troubles disappear," she said.

"Excuse me?" I cried. "What do you mean?"

"Don't worry about it," Iris replied, still smiling. "Just go home and relax. You'll be happy this time, Wade. I promise."

A few seconds later, Carl and I began our long walk home.

It felt so good to be back to normal. Not to be weighed down by a tonne of fur.

But I still felt troubled.

Disappear? I thought.

What did she mean, *make my troubles disappear*?

"Don't worry, Wade." Mum kissed me on the forehead. "Micah will take good care of you. Won't you, Micah?"

"I'll take care of her, all right," Micah said. He mussed up my hair, doing his brother act. As if he and I were great buddies.

It was the next morning, the morning after the Big Hair Crisis. Mum and Dad marched into the kitchen with a couple of suitcases and announced that they were going away overnight.

"A romantic night at the beach," Dad explained. "Just your mother and me."

"Isn't that sweet?" Mum gushed.

Adorable, I thought crankily.

I didn't mind them going away for the night. But I didn't like being left alone with Micah. Completely at his mercy. With no one to keep him from torturing me.

"Have a good time." Micah smiled. I could tell

he couldn't wait to have the place to himself. "I'll make sure Wade doesn't burn the house down."

Mum kissed him on the cheek. My stomach turned.

"We've left you a list of chores to do today." Dad pointed to a piece of paper lying on the worktop. "You can each do half the list. And don't slack off. I'll be checking the list when I get back."

I glanced at the list. It was endless!

"No parties!" Mum added, picking up her suitcase. "Micah, you can use my car if you need to. But don't stay out too late. And don't forget about your sister."

"If I had my own car—" Micah began.

"Don't start that now, Micah," Dad warned. "See you tomorrow! We'll be home early."

I watched them drive off. How can they do this to me? I wondered. How can they leave me here with Micah, spelled B-E-A-S-T.

Oh, well. Maybe it's good that they've left, I thought. They won't be here to see my revenge on Micah ... whatever it is.

I wondered what spell Iris had cast on him. When would it start working? So far, Micah seemed to be his normal, obnoxious self.

He grabbed me in a headlock. "Ready for some fun, Wade?" He tightened his grip, nearly choking me.

"L-let go!" I sputtered

He tickled me under my arms. I *hate* being tickled.

"Stop it!" I cried. I squirmed away.

Micah grabbed the list on the worktop and dangled it in front of me. "You'd better get to work on your chores. Don't forget—Dad is going to check up on you tomorrow."

"*My* chores?" I cried. "How come they're *my* chores?"

"I'm too busy," Micah replied.

"You can't make me do all these chores," I said. I shoved the list back at him. "There's no way you can make me!"

"Of course I can," he replied nastily.

"How?" I demanded shrilly.

"This little photo." Micah waved a Polaroid picture in front of my face.

"Give me that!" I demanded. "What is it?"

He held it high above my head. "Didn't you hear me sneak into your room this morning?" Micah's smile was so wide, I wanted to punch him.

"Huh? You *what*?" I screeched.

"You were sleeping like a baby," Micah said. "Snoring. In your underwear. With a little line of drool dripping out of your mouth. And I caught it all on film."

I shook with anger. I couldn't believe anyone could be so mean.

"You didn't!" I cried.

"Oh, yes, I did." Micah flashed the photo in front of me. One glimpse was enough to make my heart sink with a *THUD*.

There I was, eyes shut, mouth hanging open, drool running down my chin. In my underwear.

"Give me that!" I shouted. I made a grab for the picture. Laughing, Micah pulled it out of my reach.

"You'd better get to work. If the chores aren't done by the end of the day, Steve Wilson is going to get this glamorous photo of you in the post tomorrow."

"You creep!" I screamed. "I hate you! I hate you! I wish you'd disappear and never come back!"

That night, I got my wish.

After dinner, Micah jumped up from the table. "Clean up," he growled. "I'm going out."

"Going out?" I cried. "Where?"

He sneered at me. "That's *your* business? I don't think so." He grabbed Mum's car keys and trotted to the door. "Don't wait up."

A few seconds later, I heard him squeal down the driveway and roar away.

Carl came over after I'd finished loading the dishes into the dishwasher. "What happened to Micah?" he demanded. "Did he grow an extra arm? Does he have nose hair down to his chin?"

"*Nothing* happened," I replied. "He stubbed his toe this afternoon. That's about the worst of it."

Carl tried to make me feel better. "The spell just hasn't started working yet. I bet something really sick will happen to him tonight."

"I hope so." I sighed. "I hope so."

*

After Carl had left, I tried to wait up for Micah. But by eleven o'clock I felt very sleepy.

I kept flipping the TV remote from channel to channel. Forcing my eyes to stay open.

But at midnight I gave up and went to bed.

I turned out all the lights. Just to be mean. I hoped he'd fall or hit his head in the dark.

I fell into a restless sleep. I kept half-listening for Micah's return. Some time during the night, I had a strange dream.

In my dream I saw Maggie. A dark, blood-red light shone on her black feathers.

She flapped her wings . . . once, twice, three times—and turned into a girl. I didn't recognize the girl. I'd never seen her before.

The girl spun round three times—and turned into Iris!

I called out to Iris in my dream. *Iris! Help me!* Iris reached her arms out to me—then stopped.

She rubbed her long, shiny black hair three times—and turned into the crow! The crow opened its beak wide and let out three ear-splitting shrieks.

"YAAAAIIII!"

I woke up screaming. I sat straight up. And gulped in long breaths of air.

Whew! "What a weird dream," I murmured out loud.

Morning sunlight poured into my bedroom window. I realized I must have slept late.

Was Micah still asleep?

I climbed out of bed, dressed quickly, and made my way down the hall to Micah's room. His door was closed. I knocked.

No answer.

I knocked harder.

Nothing.

I opened the door. Micah's room was dark. I switched on the light.

The bed—empty. Still made.

He hadn't slept in it. He hadn't come home.

Had he stayed out all night without calling? He would never do that if Mum and Dad were home.

I found Micah's address book. I went downstairs and called his friends. None of them had seen him last night.

Finally, I reached Micah's best friend, Ryan. "This is Wade. Did Micah stay with you last night?" I asked.

"I didn't see him," Ryan replied. "We were supposed to meet at my house. But Micah never showed up."

Never showed up?

Cold fear squeezed my heart.

I suddenly knew what had happened.

Iris. Iris had made my troubles disappear.

Iris had made my *brother* disappear!

I stood in the middle of the kitchen, trembling, with the phone still gripped in my hand.

Micah had gone. Gone for ever.

And it was all my fault.

I started to gag. I felt sick.

And then I heard a rumbling sound. From the driveway.

A car.

I lurched to the window. Mum and Dad were home.

What do I tell them? I asked myself. What do I say?

Mum and Dad dropped their overnight bags at the back door and kissed me hello. "Where's Micah?" Dad asked.

"Uh . . . well . . ."

What do I say? Do I tell them the truth?

No. No. I can't.

"I think he went to work early," I lied. I had to stall them. Maybe I could find a way to bring him back before they found out.

Dad folded his arms. "It's Saturday, Wade," he said sternly. "Micah doesn't work on Saturday."

"Oh, wow." My heart pounded so hard, I couldn't think straight. "Uh . . . well, he went out early. Maybe he's planning a surprise for you!"

Mum glared at me. "Don't try to cover for him, Wade. He stayed out all night—*didn't* he?"

I lowered my eyes to the floor. "Well . . ."

Dad laughed. "Stayed out all night! What a boy! Think he takes after me?"

Mum gave him a playful shove. "It isn't funny. Micah was supposed to stay at home and take care of Wade."

"I'm . . . okay," I said. Another lie.

"Wait till he gets home," Mum said sharply. "I'm going to give that boy a piece of my mind."

Yeah, sure, I thought. Wait till he gets home . . .

It might be a long wait. A *very* long wait.

I started towards the door.

"Wade, where are you going?" Mum called.

"Uh . . . I have to see someone," I replied.

"You've got to bring him back—right now!" I told Iris. I paced to and fro in the tiny trailer, hands on my waist, my heart pounding.

Iris flipped back her long hair with a toss of her head. "Bring him back? Why?"

"Because—because—" I sputtered furiously.

"I thought you'd be happy," she said.

"Happy?" I shrieked. "What about my parents? What about Micah's friends? Our whole family? Everyone will be heartbroken. Our family will be ruined. No one will ever be the same!"

Iris stared at me as I paced. She shook her head. "I'm sorry. You came to me for revenge. I gave you a perfect revenge."

"It's not perfect!" I wailed. "It's horrible! Don't you even see what you've done? My brother has gone for ever—and it's all my fault! I'll never get over that. For the rest of my life—"

"What am I supposed to do?" Iris huffed. "Bring him back?"

"Yes—of course!" I screamed. "Bring him back."

She crossed her arms in front of her purple dress. "Well, sorry. I can't."

"Can't?" I cried weakly.

"It's too hard," Iris explained. "It's a very complicated spell. It took me hours. I'm not even sure I can undo it."

"But you've got to try!" I pleaded.

"I'm really sorry," Iris replied. "But I can't do it. You'll have to leave. I have a business to run here."

"I won't leave!" I insisted. I dropped into the big purple armchair against the wall. "I won't leave until you bring Micah back."

"Not possible," Iris said firmly. "Not for free. I've done all I can do for you, Wade, for free."

I stared hard at her. "You mean—"

Her dark eyes flashed. "I can bring your brother back, safe and sound. But . . . there's a price."

I swallowed hard.

I knew this was coming. Iris had warned me that sooner or later I'd have to pay her for her spells.

"Do you *really* want your brother back?" Iris asked, leaning close, her eyes suddenly gleaming with excitement. "Are you ready to pay the price?"

I had no choice.

"Okay," I sighed. "What is it, Iris? What do you want me to do?"

"I won't kid you. What I'm asking you to do is very dangerous," Iris began. "You could end up like . . . your brother."

I gasped. "You mean I could disappear too?"

She nodded.

Behind her, Maggie had been jumping from side to side on her perch. But now the crow settled down and grew silent, as if listening.

"You can leave now," Iris said softly. "You don't have to risk your life."

"Yes, I do," I replied, struggling to stop my legs from trembling. I crossed them tightly and gripped the arms of the chair. "I have to get Micah back. Tell me what I have to do."

Iris sighed. "It's your choice. Please remember that."

She cleared her throat. "I have a twin sister," she explained. "Her name is Paula. She lives in an old, abandoned house on the other side of town. It's in a nice neighbourhood, at the end of Andover Street. Maybe you know it?"

Huh? I *did* know the house she was talking about. It was in *my* neighbourhood. I passed it every day on my way to school. Such a dark and frightening place.

Carl called it "The Dead House". Not because it was full of ghosts—although it really did look haunted. But because the house itself looked dead—grey and decayed and rotting like a corpse.

"Your sister lives in that house?" I asked. "I didn't think anybody lived there."

"She lives there, all right," Iris insisted. "I haven't spoken to her in years. Because she's an evil person. But I've kept track of her. I know she's in that old house."

"Your sister . . . is evil?" I repeated.

Iris nodded solemnly. "She has the same powers I have. But she uses them for no good. She uses her powers to hurt people. She turns people into things . . . into creatures . . . into monsters . . . just for fun!"

A chill crept down my spine. "Why are you telling me about her?" I demanded.

Iris ignored my question. She shut her eyes as she continued her story.

"I used to have two crows. Maggie and her sister, Minnie. Minnie is the powerful crow. Minnie is the magical one. That's why my sister stole her!"

In the cage against the wall, Maggie cawed loudly, as if she understood Iris's story.

Iris leaned towards me. "If you want your brother back, Wade, you'll have to do me a dangerous favour. You must go across town. Sneak into my sister's house. Use your wits. Use all your cleverness—before Paula uses her evil magic on you. And *steal* Minnie back for me!"

"But . . . if I can't do it?" I started, my voice trembling with fear.

"Without Minnie," Iris replied in a whisper, "there is no way I can bring your brother back."

"But, when—?" I choked out.

Iris tugged me up from the chair and pushed me to the door. "Go now," she urged. "Go now, Wade. My sister sleeps during the day. So she can do her evil magic all night."

I stepped out on to the paved ground. "But, Iris," I started. "If I get caught . . ."

"Good luck."

She slammed the trailer door shut.

I stopped at Carl's house. I planned to beg him to come with me to the creepy old house.

But he wasn't at home. His mum reminded me that Carl has Little League every Saturday morning.

So I was on my own.

As I walked the two blocks, my heart pounded and my legs trembled as if they were rubber.

"You can't turn back," I told myself. "You have to do it. You *have* to."

I forced my way up to the tall hedge in front of the abandoned house.

It was a bright, sunny morning. But tall, old trees tilting over the house cast it in deep shadow. A huge tree had fallen in the centre of the garden. Branches rotting, bark peeling, it sprawled in the tall weeds like a decaying skeleton.

A torn shutter banged against one side of the house. Along the front wall, all of the windows were shattered. The roof sagged in the middle. A pile of old newspapers formed a grey mound on the porch.

No signs of life.

I took a deep breath. Then keeping in the long shadows, I crept across the weed-strewn garden. Up to the front porch.

Swarms of black ants crawled over the broken concrete. I stepped carefully round the yellowed pile of old newspapers. Up to the door.

How do I get into this place? I asked.

I can't just ring the bell.

My head was spinning. I suddenly felt dizzy. From fear.

I pressed both hands against the door to keep myself from tumbling over. And the door creaked open.

Dark inside. The tall trees didn't allow any sunlight to filter down.

I leaned into the front hallway. No one in sight.

The sour smell of dust and mould and decay greeted me. What a disgusting odour—so thick, I started to choke.

Holding my breath, I stepped into the house.

And something sticky wrapped round my face.

"Ohhhh!" I gasped. Cobwebs?

Yes. I tugged them off my skin with both hands.

I peered round. Cobwebs floated from the walls like ghosts.

I took a step. Then another. The floorboards creaked beneath my shoes.

I can't do this, I realized.

I'm too afraid. I can barely move.

There's no way I can steal the crow and get away from here without being caught.

"*Paula turns people into creatures,*" Iris said. "*She turns people into . . . monsters.*"

Where *is* Paula? I wondered.

I wrapped my arms round myself to stop myself shaking. I took a deep breath. And then another. And then I stepped into a long, dark hall.

Cobwebs brushed against my face, my arms. I ignored them and stared straight ahead, letting my eyes adjust to the dark.

I saw doorways on both sides of the hall, all of them dark. At the far end, a pale rectangle of light poured on to the floor from an open door.

Still hugging myself, I forced my rubbery legs to move. I made my way slowly, step by step, down the dark hallway. Halfway to the lighted room at the end, I stopped. And listened.

Where are you, Minnie? I asked silently.

Flutter your wings. Caw for me. Please. Give me a clue.

Silence. The only sound—my own shallow breathing.

With a sigh, I crept the rest of the way.

I stepped into the rectangle of light on the floor.

And stopped again.

I peered into the open doorway. A curtain of silvery cobwebs hung halfway down the door.

I bent down to see beyond the thick webs. But I couldn't see much. Dark curtains over a dust-covered window. Peeling grey wallpaper.

Are you in there, Minnie? I wondered.

Caw now! Please—make a noise!

No. Not a sound.

I took another deep breath. And stepped up to the door.

I ducked under the cobwebs. Crept into the room.

And gasped.

My eyes swept past the broken furniture, the stained carpet thick with dust. The light bulb hanging on a long wire from the cracked ceiling.

I stared at the birdcage, on the mantelpiece against the far wall.

Minnie!

The crow swung on a swing inside the small wire cage. It tilted its head as I entered the room, and kept swinging.

Yes! The sight of the bird cheered me up. Gave me hope.

So close. The crow was so close. I could grab it and race out—

A loud cough made me scream out loud.

I clapped both hands over my mouth—and turned towards the sound.

A black armchair in front of the mantel. The leather chair had torn yellow stuffing pouring out.

In the armchair—a sleeping figure.

Was she sleeping? I couldn't really tell. Her long black hair completely covered her face.

Paula.

She wore a purple dress, just like her sister. One arm dangled over the side of the chair. Her head tilted forward. It bobbed slowly, rhythmically.

She's snoring, I realized.

She *is* asleep!

I squinted hard, trying to see her face. But the long tangles of black hair covered it like a heavy drape.

I stood perfectly still for a while, watching her head rock gently up and down, listening to her soft snores.

Okay, Wade, she's asleep, I told myself.

This shouldn't be too hard. Cross the room. Grab the birdcage. And get out of here as fast as you can.

Yes, it seemed easy. But suddenly, as I made my way to the mantel, the birdcage seemed a *mile* away.

I took a step and then another.

The wooden floorboards squeaked noisily.

In her armchair, Paula stirred. She groaned.

My knees started to collapse. I nearly fell to the floor.

Take it easy! I ordered myself.

I watched Paula's head bob. Sound asleep again.

I'll *slide* across the floor, I decided. Maybe then the floorboards won't squeak.

I shuffled slowly, carefully across the room.

When I made it to the cage, I was trembling so hard I grabbed the mantel to hold myself up.

And the whole thing started to topple over!

No! I shoved it up—and pressed my shoulder against it.

The mantel rested against the wall.

The crow tilted its head, watching me with its glimmering black eyes. It fluttered its feathers.

"Ssshhh," I whispered.

I lifted the cage off the mantel. It was heavier than I thought.

I gripped the cage with both hands.

Turned silently. And began shuffling once again, sliding my shoes over the old floorboards.

Almost there, I thought, my eyes on the open doorway.

I'm almost out of here.

I was halfway across the room when I heard a rustling behind me. A cough.

I turned in time to see Paula jump up from her chair.

She bolted across the room to block my way.

"Where do you think *you're* going?" she cried.

I let out a scream.

The cage fell from my hands. It clattered against the floor. Bounced twice.

The crow squawked and frantically beat its wings.

The cage came to a rest on its side.

"Who *are* you?" Paula screeched.

"I—I—I—" I couldn't speak.

She stepped up close to me. And then she raised both hands to the long black hair that covered her face.

With a quick motion, she slid the hair away from her face, like sliding heavy curtains open.

I stared at her face. Stared. Stared in horror and disbelief—and screamed again.

"Micah—!" I cried. "Micah! It's *you*! You—you—!"

My terror quickly turned to fury. What kind of hideous, horrible joke was this?

He threw back his head and laughed.

Laughed long and hard, bending over and slapping his knees beneath the purple dress.

Then he raised both hands. Tugged off the black wig—and heaved it at me.

The wig bounced off my chest and landed next to the birdcage. The crow cawed loudly in protest.

"What—what are you *doing* here?" I finally choked out in a high, shrill voice.

"Waiting for you," he replied, grinning a disgusting, triumphant grin.

"I—I came here to *save* you!" I cried.

"I know!" he grinned. "That's the best part!"

I uttered a sob. "You mean—? You mean—?"

I stared at his grinning face. I wanted to punch him and punch him and punch him until he stopped grinning.

Why was he here? Who gave him the crow and the wig and the purple dress?

"Did Iris—?" I started. I was too furious to speak.

"Iris set it all up," Micah explained, the grin finally fading. He tugged at the front of the dress. "She gave me this and the wig and everything."

"And she sent me here so that you could scare me?" I demanded.

Micah nodded. "Yes. That was my revenge."

I gaped at him, my whole body shaking. "Excuse me?"

"Don't you get it, Wade?" he said. "It was *all* my revenge."

I just stared at him. I couldn't think. I couldn't speak.

His revenge? How could it be Micah's revenge?

"I saw the magazine ad on your dressing-table," Micah explained. "Thank goodness I decided to snoop around in your room! I saw the ad—and I knew you would use it on me. So I went to Iris first!"

"You—you—" I shook my fist at him.

This couldn't be happening. It *couldn't*!

"Remember the itching, Wade?" Micah continued. "Remember the hair growing and growing?"

"How could I forget it?" I moaned.

"Well, Iris didn't mess up," Micah explained gleefully. "She cast those spells on you *on purpose*!"

"Oh, noooo!" I wailed.

Micah laughed. "You thought you were getting revenge. But it was *my* revenge the whole time!"

"And Minnie?" I cried weakly, pointing at the crow. "Paula and Minnie?"

"A phony story," Micah sneered. "There is no Paula. And that's just an ordinary crow from a pet shop. No powers at all. But it sure fooled you."

"Yes, it did," I confessed sadly.

I suddenly felt so weak. Weak and tired.

And defeated.

"Why?" I asked him, my voice shaking. "Why did Iris do this to me?"

Micah sneered again. "Because I paid her, of course. I paid her three hundred dollars. Half the money I made this summer."

A long, weary sigh escaped my throat. "You win," I murmured sadly. "You win, Micah."

"I suppose I do!" he exclaimed. He tilted back his head and shouted a long victory cry.

"I'm wonderful! Aren't I wonderful? I'm so happy, I could do a back flip!" he cried.

But he didn't do a back flip. Instead, he slapped me on the back as hard as he could. And tore out of the room.

I heard him laughing and cheering all the way down the long hall and out of the house.

I suppose he has a lot to cheer about, I told myself glumly.

I'm a loser.

A real loser.

I lifted the birdcage off the floor. The crow squawked and flapped its wings.

"A loser," I muttered to myself.

Or *am* I?

Suddenly, I had an idea.

One last idea. One last, *very good* idea.

101

26

"Micah? Are you down there? Can I see you for a second?"

It was two days after that horrible scene in the abandoned house. Mum and Dad were away for the day. Micah was in charge once again.

I kneeled at the top of the stairs. I held the crow in my hands. And I called down to my brother.

"Micah? Can I see you?"

I heard him walking around down there. I petted the crow and waited.

A few seconds later, Micah appeared at the bottom of the stairs. He stared up at me angrily. "What's your problem, Wade? I'm busy."

"I just wanted to show you something," I said.

"Show me *what*? Did you learn to wave bye-bye?"

Micah laughed at his own stupid joke. But his expression changed when he saw the crow in my hands.

He scowled up at me. "What are you doing with that stupid bird? Do Mum and Dad know you brought it into the house?"

"No. But—"

"They won't let you keep it," he said nastily. "I'm going to tell them you're hiding it up there."

"I just want to show you something," I repeated. "Remember the other day? In the abandoned old house?"

He laughed. "I'll never forget it! Greatest day of my life!"

"Well . . . remember you said you wanted to do a back flip?"

He nodded. "Yeah. So what?"

I closed my eyes. I rubbed the crow's back three times.

"Go ahead, Micah," I said. "Do some back flips."

Micah laughed again. He shook his head. He sneered at me.

"What is this, Wade? *Pretend* time? That stupid crow can't help you—"

"AWWWWWK!" A strained cry burst from Micah's throat. His eyes bulged. His arms shot out.

He did an awkward back flip. Head over heels.

His legs buckled as he landed. But he caught his balance.

"Huh?" His mouth hung open in shock. He shook his head hard.

103

"Do another one," I said. "In fact, keep doing them all day."

"No! Wait!" he protested.

His hands shot up above his head. His back arched.

WHOOOOP!

Micah did another back flip.

Once again, he landed shakily. I could see the shock on his face. His whole head turned beet-red.

"Wait—" he gasped.

His arms flew up. He leaned back. He flipped again.

And then again.

Now I was laughing. *Finally*, it was my turn to laugh!

"Guess what, Micah?" I called down. I waited until he finished his next flip. Then I told him the rest:

"I sneaked back to Iris's trailer yesterday. When she went out, I crept inside and switched crows. I have the real one now. I have Maggie."

"Please—" Micah begged.

He did another back flip. And then another.

And then the front doorbell rang.

I hurried down the stairs to answer it.

"Let me stop!" Micah begged. "You've had your revenge. Please, Wade—"

He was back-flipping in front of the door, blocking my way.

The doorbell rang again.

I shoved Micah into the living-room and pulled open the door.

"Carl—hi!" I cried. "Come in."

"What's up?" Carl asked. He stepped inside—and stared open-mouthed as Micah did another back flip.

Micah landed with a loud groan. "Please, Wade—" he begged.

He did another flip.

"Why is he doing that?" Carl asked. He adjusted his glasses on his nose. He probably thought he was seeing things!

I held up the crow. "I have Maggie," I explained. "I'm finally getting a little revenge."

"Cool," Carl replied.

Micah flipped again. He crashed into a coffee-table, knocking over a china vase.

"Be careful!" I snapped. "Watch what you're doing!"

Carl and I both laughed.

This was nasty. But it was also really funny.

And it wasn't as nasty as what Micah had done to me.

"How did you get the crow?" Carl asked.

"Stole her," I replied. "Well, actually, I traded her for another crow."

Carl's smile faded. "Won't Iris come after you?"

"She can't," I replied. "She has no idea where I live. I never told her the address."

We watched Micah flip a few more times. His face was bright-red and dripping with sweat. He was wheezing loudly, groaning and moaning with each flip.

"This is getting kind of boring," I sighed. "Let's try something else."

"Yeah. Cool," Carl said. "Like what?"

I raised Maggie in front of me. "Hmmm . . ." I thought hard.

My eyes went to the window. I could see Mum's garden outside.

"I wonder if I can use Maggie to turn Micah into another kind of creature," I said, thinking out loud.

"You mean, like an animal or something?" Carl asked.

Micah groaned and did another painful back flip.

"I was thinking about an insect," I replied. I couldn't keep a smile from spreading across my face. "Or a garden slug," I told Carl. "You know. Those fat, slimy slugs in Mum's garden?"

"Go ahead. Give it a try," Carl urged.

"No!" Micah begged breathlessly. "Wade—please!"

I shut my eyes and rubbed Maggie's back once, twice . . . three times.

When I opened my eyes, Micah had vanished.

I blinked. "Oh, wow!" I cried. "He's—gone!"

"No. Look!" Carl ran into the living-room. He pointed excitedly at the carpet. "You did it, Wade! Look!"

I saw a shiny spot on the rug. No. Wait. Not a shiny spot.

A slug.

Micah, spelled S-L-U-G. Leaving a trail of white slime behind him as he inched forward.

"Oh, wow!" I saw it—but I didn't believe it.

I'd waited a long time for this revenge. And I had to go through some scary times. But it was all worth it.

I handed the crow to Carl. Then I got down on my hands and knees and lowered my face really close to the slug.

"How does it feel, Micah?" I called down to him. "How does it feel to be all wet and slimy?"

I stared down at him. I kind of expected him to answer.

But of course he couldn't make a sound. He was a slug.

"You're really ugly now," I told him. "Bet you miss your hair—huh?"

Micah slid along the carpet, leaving a thin slime trail behind him.

"Bet you miss being the big shot boss, huh?" I called down to him. "Well—get used to it. I'm in charge now, Sluggo. I've got the crow. That means you're in my control from now on!"

I wondered if Micah could hear me. I wondered if he could still understand English.

I pulled myself up. Carl stared down at Micah, shaking his head. "Maybe you should change him back," he murmured. "This is really too nasty. And it's a bit dangerous, isn't it?"

"Dangerous?" I replied. "You mean, we could lose him? Or maybe step on him?"

Carl nodded.

"Okay," I agreed. I took the crow back from Carl. "Let's turn him into something else. Something a little more fun. You pick something. It's your turn."

"How about a frog?" Carl suggested.

"Okay. Great! A frog it is!" I exclaimed. "We can make him hop down all the stairs."

"Yeah. And we can make him eat flies," Carl added.

"How great is this?" I declared. "I love revenge!"

I raised Maggie in front of me and shut my eyes. I wished for Micah to become a green, hopping frog. And I rubbed Maggie's back three times.

Carl and I stared down at the fat slug on the carpet. And as we stared, it started to grow.

It took only a few seconds for Micah to go from slug to frog. His long tongue shot out. He stared up at us with those wet, bulging frog eyes.

"He looks so sad!" I exclaimed. And burst out laughing.

"That's the saddest frog I've ever seen," Carl agreed.

"Don't be sad," I told Micah. "Or else I'll turn you into something worse!" I gave him a little push. "Start hopping. Let's see you hop!"

"*Wee-beep, wee-beep*." He croaked out a loud protest. But then he took a few short hops across the rug.

I was about to give him another push—when the doorbell rang.

"Who can that be?" I cried. I climbed to my feet, made my way to the door and pulled it open.

"Iris!" I gasped.

She stared at me angrily, tossing her black

109

hair behind her shoulders. "Wade—I believe you have something of mine," she growled.

I tried to slam the door.

But she lowered her shoulder—and pushed her way into the house.

She was breathing hard. Her normally pale face was red with anger. Her dark eyes flared.

"How—how did you find me?" I choked out. "I never told you the address."

"Your brother paid me with a cheque," she explained. "Your address was on the cheque." She lowered her eyes to Maggie.

The bird cawed loudly and fluttered its wings.

"Where *is* your brother, Wade?" Iris demanded.

"Well . . ." I pointed to the frog on the living-room carpet.

"I warned you not to mess with Maggie," Iris growled. "Didn't I warn you?"

I nodded. "Yes, but I had to have my revenge. You cheated me, Iris. You—"

Her features tightened. She glared at me with cold menace.

"Stealing is a very serious crime, Wade," she snarled. "Hand me the crow. I'm going to have to teach you a very serious lesson."

"No—please!" I cried.

But Iris moved quickly. With a loud cry, she leapt forward—and swiped the crow from my hands.

Iris raised Maggie in front of her face. "I warned you, Wade," she repeated coldly. "You shouldn't fool around with powers you don't know anything about."

"Please, Iris," I pleaded. "I'm sorry I took your crow. But I had to. I—"

"Silence!" she shrieked.

Carl and I both took a step back.

"You must be taught that stealing is wrong," Iris said. She gazed down at Micah. "I know what I'll do. I'll let you join your brother down on the floor."

"You mean—turn me into a frog?" I gasped.

Iris nodded. "I'll turn you *and* your friend into frogs. I don't want you to be lonely."

"Hey!" Carl cried. "What did *I* do? I didn't steal your crow!"

"Don't hurt Carl!" I cried. "He didn't do anything. Really!"

"I hope that you all have learned a lesson

about revenge," Iris said. "And that lesson is . . . revenge is sweet. But you shouldn't try it at home. You should always leave it to the professionals."

"Iris—please! Please don't!" I begged again.

"Please don't turn us into frogs!" Carl pleaded.

But she shut her eyes. And started to rub the crow's back.

I watched her rub Maggie once. Twice . . .

And then I leapt forward—and grabbed the crow from her hands.

Iris uttered a startled cry and opened her eyes. She swiped both hands at Maggie, trying to grab her back. But I staggered away from her, holding the crow tightly.

"I'm sorry, Iris," I cried. "But I can't let you turn us into frogs."

I lifted the crow.

Iris raised her hands to her cheeks. "What are you going to do?" she demanded.

"I guess I'm going to get my revenge on you too," I told her.

"Wade—I'm warning you—" Iris started. "Don't—"

But I didn't want to give her a chance to grab Maggie back.

I shut my eyes. I wished for Iris to turn into

a frog. And I rubbed Maggie's back once, twice
. . . three times.

I opened my eyes to find Iris staring at me in
horror. "What have you done?" she cried.

"Turned you into a frog," I told her.

"But you don't know the rules!" she protested.
"I warned you. There are rules."

I sneered at her. "What rules?"

"Did you know that you can only make *three*
wishes a day on Maggie? Did you know that if
you make a *fourth* wish, it gets turned on to
you?"

"Huh?" I gasped. "Only three wishes?"

"How many wishes have you made today,
Wade?" Iris demanded.

"Uh . . . well . . ."

I counted them silently to myself:

1) Back flips for Micah
2) Micah into a slug
3) Micah into a frog

"How many have you made?" Iris asked again.
"Tell me, Wade. How many?"

Her voice suddenly sounded so far away.

"*Wee-beep*," I replied. "*Wee-beep, wee-beeeep*."

And I hopped across the rug to join my
brother. Maybe I *won't* get revenge on Iris after
all, I thought.

I saw a juicy fly on the wall beside the sofa.
Yum. It seemed a lot more important than any
stupid revenge.

Welcome to the new millennium of fear

Check out this chilling preview
of what's next from
R.L. Stine

Fright Camp

"Camp meeting in the lodge!" a green-uniformed counsellor called out. "All campers to the lodge!"

Kids came jogging in from all directions. I waved to Jack and Chris as I made my way through the open doorway.

The front of the lodge was built to look like a log cabin. But the building was actually two storeys tall and as big as a barn.

To the left, I could see a row of small rooms down a long hallway. We were herded into an enormous room with wooden rafters along the ceiling and tall stone fireplaces on both ends. Long wooden tables filled the centre of the room. A sign proclaimed: MESS HALL & MEETING ROOM.

Movie posters of R.B. Farraday films were hung along one wall. I recognized *The Beast with Three Brains* and *Kunga, the Animal Vampire*.

The counsellors motioned for us to sit at the long tables. I found a seat in the second row of tables next to some older-looking boys.

I started to say something to them. But a tall, athletic-looking counsellor stepped in front of us. "Both hands on the tables, everyone," he instructed. "Fast. Hands on the tables."

"Whoa!" I uttered a startled cry as he pulled up heavy black cords from under the table—and strapped them round our wrists.

"Handcuffs?" one of the other kids cried.

"Are we under arrest?" someone called.

We all laughed at that.

But I felt a little strange as counsellors moved quickly along the tables, strapping down everyone's hands.

And a chill tingled the back of my neck as I felt a hum of electricity run through the black cords.

"What is *this* about?" I asked the boy next to me.

He shrugged. "It's pretty weird," he muttered.

I tugged at the cords. They were fastened tight. I couldn't slip free.

Again, I felt a hum of electricity round my wrists.

I turned and glanced behind me. I saw Meredith and Elizabeth at the next table. Their wrists were strapped down. They were chatting excitedly, both talking at once.

In the row behind them, I saw Chris struggling with the counsellors. "No way!" he shouted. "No way!"

He wrapped his hands behind his back and jumped to his feet. "You can't do this!" he cried angrily.

But three counsellors held Chris down. They pulled his hands apart and strapped his wrists. "A troublemaker," one of the counsellors said. "What's your name? We're going to remember you."

"I don't believe this," I muttered to the boy next to me. "Why is Chris so frightened?"

The boy shrugged. "Beats me."

I didn't have long to think about it. A big, tough-looking man in a white lab coat stepped to the front of the room. He raised two enormous hands to silence us.

"Welcome—prisoners!" he bellowed.

We all laughed. Uncomfortable laughter.

Two counsellors rushed up to him. They both pointed to Chris. The man in the lab coat stared long and hard at Chris.

The man had cold grey eyes and a broad, bulbous nose that looked as if it had been broken several times. He was nearly bald. A dark scar started at one eyebrow and trailed up along his forehead.

He raised his hands until the room grew silent. "My name is Alonso," he announced. "I am the assistant warden."

Warden? Prisoners?

What's going on here? I wondered.

But then I saw a smile spread over Alonso's face. His grey eyes twinkled. "Welcome to Fright Camp, everyone!" he declared. He rubbed his hands together. "We are going to do our best to give you some good scares this summer."

"Why are our hands strapped down?" a boy demanded in an angry, trembling voice. I turned and saw that it was Jack.

"Yeah! Let us go!" Chris cried angrily. "You can't do this! Let us go!"

I felt a tingle of electricity against my wrists.

Alonso glared at my two bunk mates. "What are your names?" he demanded.

Jack and Chris didn't reply.

"Your names?" Alonso repeated, lumbering towards them menacingly.

The two boys called out their names.

"And what cabin are you in?" Alonso asked.

They both hesitated. "Cabin Three," Chris told him finally.

A strange, unpleasant grin spread over Alonso's face. The scar on his forehead throbbed. "That will be our *lucky* cabin," he declared coldly.

Alonso turned and strode back to the front of the room. "I have a wonderful treat for you now," he announced in his deep, booming voice. "I have the pleasure of introducing the owner of Fright Camp. His thirty-five movies have won him the title of the Scariest Man on Earth! Let's give a big Fright Camp welcome to R.B. Farraday!"

I tried to clap, but the tight cords round my wrists made it hard. So I cheered instead.

We all cheered and screamed as R.B. Farraday shuffled into the room. I heard a few kids gasp in surprise. He wasn't the way we pictured him.

For one thing, he was very short. He only came up to Alonso's shoulders. He wasn't just short. He was tiny. A small, slender head topped with slicked-down black hair. A closely trimmed black beard with a streak of grey down the centre.

He wore a black T-shirt, black shorts, and sandals. His legs were as skinny as toothpicks. So were his arms.

I saw something sparkle against the front of his shirt. Squinting, I saw that it was a silvery skull on a chain, with glittering red eyes.

I leant over the table, staring at him. My hero! The most famous horror director on Earth. I couldn't believe I was in the same room as he was!

Mr Farraday pulled himself on to a tall wooden stool. He had a clipboard in one hand. He scratched his beard with the other hand, waiting for our cheers to stop.

"Thank you for the warm welcome," he said finally. I leant forward, straining to listen. He had a soft, almost whispery voice.

"This is an exciting summer for me," he continued. He spread the clipboard across his bony knees. "As Alonso told you, I've made thirty-five movies. But that's only film. Colour images on celluloid. This camp gives me a chance to bring my movies to life. And now, you will all be actors!"

We cheered again.

The cords tugged at my wrist. "Why are we wearing these?" I called out.

Several other kids chimed in. The big room echoed with our questions.

Alonso signalled sternly for us to be quiet.

But Mr Farraday rubbed his beard and smiled. "Have any of you seen my film *The Revenge of Dr Cruel*?" he asked.

Several kids cried out yes.

"Then you will recognize the Fear Meter," Mr Farraday said. "These wires connect all of you to the actual Fear Meter that was used in the movie."

"But—what does it do?" a girl called from the front row.

"I will show you," Mr Farraday replied. He slid down from the stool and turned to Alonso. "Why don't you pick a volunteer."

Alonso rumbled up to the tables. He fiddled with the cuffs of his white lab coat. His grey eyes swept back and forth over the room.

He really looks like an evil doctor in one of R.B. Farraday's movies, I thought.

I hadn't seen *The Revenge of Dr Cruel* in a long time. I struggled to remember exactly what the Fear Meter did.

Alonso raised a big hand and pointed. "Let's demonstrate on that one," Alonso said. "One of the troublemakers."

"No!" I heard Chris scream. "No—not me!" He struggled to free his hands from the cords. "Please! Not me!"

Why is he so afraid? I wondered.

Kids shifted and squirmed. All eyes were on Chris now.

I caught the frightened expressions on Elizabeth's and Meredith's faces. Behind them, Jack had his eyes shut tight.

I turned back to the front and saw Mr Farraday push some buttons on a control panel. Then he threw a big switch on the wall.

"Nooooo!" Chris gasped.

I heard a sharp crackle of electricity.

Chris jerked hard in his seat.

His head snapped back.

He jumped up. His whole body twisted and danced.

Another hard jolt of electricity.

Kids screamed. Horrified cries shook the room.

I let out a laugh. "It's a joke," I told the boy next to me. "It's got to be a joke."

But Chris's head snapped to one side. And then his whole body collapsed.

He crumpled on to the table and didn't move.

"Shut it down! Shut it down!" Mr Farraday screamed. He fiddled frantically with the control buttons.

Alonso leant over Chris and shook him by the shoulders.

Some kids screamed. Others stared in silence. I gasped for breath, my heart pounding, watching Alonso try to revive Chris.

"Is he okay?" Mr Farraday demanded. "Is he alive?"

"He'll survive," Alonso replied coldly. He motioned to two counsellors. "Take him out of here."

Alonso loosened the straps. The two counsellors lifted Chris's limp body from the seat. They had a lot of trouble pulling him up and almost dropped him.

No one uttered a sound as the counsellors carried Chris from the room. The door closed hard behind them.

Mr Farraday rubbed his beard and paced back and forth in front of the fireplace. He motioned for Alonso to join him.

"We'd better turn down the voltage for the next group," Mr Farraday told his assistant, shaking his head.

Alonso rubbed his hands together. An evil smile crossed his face. "It's more fun this way!" he declared.

Mr Farraday stopped pacing and stared at him. "You're too evil, Alonso. Don't make me sorry I hired you for this job."